THAT
SAVAGE
WATER

THAT SAVAGE WATER

STORIES

MATTHEW R. LONEY

EXILE
editions

Library and Archives Canada Cataloguing in Publication

Loney, Matthew R., author
That savage water : stories / Matthew R. Loney.

Issued in print and electronic formats.
ISBN 978-1-55096-413-4 (pbk.).--ISBN 978-1-55096-416-5 (pdf).--
ISBN 978-1-55096-414-1 (epub).--ISBN 978-1-55096-415-8 (mobi)

I. Title

PS8623.O523T43 2014   C813'.6   C2014-902989-6
                                              C2014-902990-X

Design and Composition by Mishi Uroboros
Cover concept by Matthew R. Loney
Typeset in Big Caslon and Hellas Fun fonts at Moons of Jupiter Studios

Published by Exile Editions Ltd ~ www.ExileEditions.com
144483 Southgate Road 14 – GD, Holstein, Ontario, N0G 2A0
Printed and Bound in Canada in 2014, by Imprimerie Gauvin

We gratefully acknowledge, for their support toward our publishing
activities, the Canada Council for the Arts, the Government of Canada
through the Canada Book Fund (CBF), the Ontario Arts Council,
and the Ontario Media Development Corporation.

Conseil des Arts du Canada   **Canada Council for the Arts**   Canada

ONTARIO ARTS COUNCIL
CONSEIL DES ARTS DE L'ONTARIO
an Ontario government agency
un organisme du gouvernement de l'Ontario

Ontario
Ontario Media Development Corporation

Canadian Sales: The Canadian Manda Group, 165 Dufferin Street,
Toronto ON M6K 3H6   www.mandagroup.com   416 516 0911

North American and International Distribution, and U.S. Sales:
Independent Publishers Group, 814 North Franklin Street,
Chicago IL 60610   www.ipgbook.com   toll free: 1 800 888 4741

for those who never made it
to the surface

THAT SAVAGE WATER

Out where the eastern bank of the Ganges curved into a broad, alluvial sand belt, the backs of the melon farmers arched in broken parabolas over the low-lying foliage. Silhouetted against the sky, the women's saris blew out behind them like the curtains of forgotten attic windows. Closer, tourists in wooden boats clustered off the western shore. They drifted in front of the ghats, raising a bulwark of Nikons in time to catch the bathers dip beneath the surface and then rise with vigorous two-handed scrubs of their faces. Oars cradled themselves patiently in the roughened palms of the rowers; the water lapped against their hulls, a pacifist. Dawn in Varanasi always yielded spectacular photos.

Five months ago, Sal had woken before dawn for the same reason. The air, he remembered, smelled of burning hair and open sewer just enlivened by the sun. Whole families, undressed or fully clothed, descended into the Ganges on stone stairways flanking the shoreline. Grime floated past them in gelatinous layers. Petrified in the thick water, broken garlands of marigolds rode atop submerged plastic bags; ruptured shadows of rotten fruit hovered just beneath the surface. Perched on the wooden seat, eager with his camera, Sal too had been rowed out onto the holy river to catch the sunrise cascade off the bathers' bodies. How long ago that morning seemed, his first in Varanasi.

Today, however, he'd felt confident enough to ask the boatman in broken Hindi to row past the barrier of tourist boats out to the far bank where the melon farmers were already tending to the sandy fields. The face of the rower, once measled by acne, was stretched over by a taut jaw of grey whiskers. He wobbled his head in acceptance of the price Sal offered and pushed the boat away from the ghat, leaping aboard with silent, feline agility. Perhaps it was because death was so exposed in this city – the perpetual funeral of an eternal cataclysm – that the residents appeared at peace in their daily suffering and survival. Aghori sadhus, members of the most extreme of the ascetic sects, roamed the cremation grounds and ate from bowls made of human skulls. Naked, their hair matted like a mongrel's, they wandered the ghats or sat meditating next to funeral pyres, their bodies coated white with the ashen remains. Death smelled a different colour here.

Sal watched the curls of water surge against the hull with the rhythm of the rower's pulls. Marigold petals spiraled in orange mandalas over the particled surface. He'd seen what went into the Ganges. Riding back in the dark from visiting with Vaman, the pyres had burned on the shore like beacons. Dead bodies shifted into detonations of sparks as the logs cracked and flames shot skyward into the full moon. Vaman was right. All was delusional attachment to temporary sense pleasures; sooner or later, the body would disintegrate. He knew that now. The news over the last two days had confirmed it for him.

Nearly every day Sal had crossed the Ganges to meet with Vaman. Some intangible wisdom encircled the young vairagi, and his words clung to the fractures in Sal's psyche like warm, soothing pulp.

—*Once one becomes a master of self* - Vaman offered Sal a tangerine - *one becomes a master of life. This cage of the self is what is making our life so limited! How important to do away with all this nonsense.*

Vaman's face seemed incapable of a frown. His expression was balanced in equanimity - the object of his meditations - but was not devoid of compassion. Confident, he spoke with an envious assurance that overrode any doubts Sal had about his age. A coarse beard roughened the young ascetic's chin and cheeks; his hair fell in tatted cords to his bare shoulders, and two lines of red streaked across his forehead. An ignorant question from Sal brought only a curious glint to Vaman's eyes, followed by a devastatingly practical answer.

The bank was already beginning to fill with families who came to the far side of the Ganges to picnic and escape the pestilent crush of the city. Doubling itself in its reflection, a white pony stood in the shallows and nosed down to its ripples to drink. Boys kicked up glittering fans of spray as they sprinted into the river and then dove beneath the surface - the offspring of the melon farmers who seemed so at home on this temporary embankment. When the monsoons arrived, the water would submerge the shore and they would exodus into the city to set up equally temporary shacks in abandoned alleyways. Having nothing meant freedom, Sal thought. It meant liberation.

—You don't want this? – the guesthouse owner asked when Sal offered him his backpack – What's the problem, man? Where you going to put your clothings anyway?

—Won't need any clothes. Just one pair, what I'm wearing.

—No clothings, sure, sure – the man unzipped the bag and peered inside – No shoes too?

—Don't need those either.

—What you going to do anyway, huh, no-shoes?

The blades of the ceiling fan cut across the TV screen in the upper corner of the room. An Indian newscaster was reporting from the southeastern coast. In continual playback from shaky cameras, an enormous wave rushed into shore flooding the streets, cracking buildings, sweeping vehicles away. Upside-down fishing boats pursued men clinging to palm trunks. Intercut with women wailing in Tamil, the survivors picked through the rubble searching for remnants of their children. Indonesia had been hit the hardest. South Thailand and Sri Lanka were destroyed. Burma was a black, suspicious silence. The rocketing death toll convinced Sal even more.

—*You may not even have the opportunity to enjoy what you are working so hard for* – Vaman had said – *Everyday people's efforts are to acquire things that will most certainly vanish. What devastation! What devastation for the soul.*

—I keep the bag for when you come back - the owner's eyes were fixed.

—I won't come back - Sal said.

—Sure sure, no-shoes-man. Think you are the first white guy to come to India and meet a guru? I'm Dalit but I'm Dravidian also. That means I'm no dummy! I keep the bag for when you come back.

—Thailand got hit too? - in the cool of a corner chair, an Australian backpacker slumped slack-jawed at the screen - Jesus, imagine that. All those tourist resorts on Phuket. *Wham!* A ton of dead foreigners on vacation.

Sal turned to leave - They all ran down to the beach to watch the wave.

He felt a tug tighten against him like an undertow. The ceiling fan sliced across the news anchor's face. It too would disintegrate.

To the left of the melon fields on a curve in the embankment where the Ganges turtles laid their eggs, Vaman's hut was a driftwood construction of scraps of tattered fabric. Perfect in its poverty, the sadhu's surroundings had intrigued Sal on his first trip to the far banks: a few oranges nested in a frayed basket, stacks of cow manure for a simple fire, a shrine to Rama, the Lord of self-control. Across the river, Varanasi swarmed while Vaman sat cross-legged, his eyes closed, chanting bhajans - a tranquil oasis opposite a flurry of death.

The desolation of the sandbank reminded Sal of an island tearing free of the mainland, a giant beach-raft of contented castaways riding farther from the chaotic shore. He felt nervous, as though if he lingered too long the city would disappear and he'd be caught adrift. Sal studied Vaman for some time before the sadhu finally broke from his meditation to stoke the fire.

—I was just curious – Sal raised his hand at the sadhu who spotted him – I'm sorry.

—*You are on Krishna's land, not mine* – Vaman replied – *You need not make apology for that.*

For a moment, Sal thought the man was a Westerner. He'd seen them in Delhi and Rishikesh, dread-locked foreigners in loincloths with begging bowls, pale-skinned disciples who'd grown tired of office politics, mortgages and dress socks, choosing instead to live in caves smoking hashish, owning nothing. How must it feel to leave everything behind? To pick up and walk away and start again?

—*Nature is the best teacher for us humans* – the sadhu broke a disc of manure and dropped the halves on the fire – *So easily it can show you the state of your spirit, yes? Come and look here. Look here at this fire.*

Sal came to the flames, a few bright sticks ignited against the dawn.

The sadhu spoke – *If I am in sorrow, I will see that this fire contains sorrow, no? Or this river. To those who are not wanting to clean their hearts, it seems a filthy river. Yet to those who come seeking purification, it instantly becomes the Holy Ganges. Everything, you see, depends upon the vantage you are looking. But this takes time to understand. Much time!*

There are no shortcuts for this thinking – As though he expected a response, he lifted his bony face to look at Sal.

He could think of none except – Right. No shortcuts.

Vaman continued – *Many people are now coming to India to learn meditation, to learn yoga. First, they lose themselves at the beach parties and then find themselves at yoga. In such an order it always happens. After, they go home to their countries and they want to make a school, to ask for money from students. Such a brilliant experience they had in India, they will tell you, so sure of enlightenment. After only these few lessons, maybe fifteen days or one month, they feel they can become a teacher!*

The sadhu laughed. It reverberated like the wisest laugh Sal had ever heard, a lustrous, intelligent ripple that shocked the guru's eyes into brilliant sparks.

Sal went to the train station that night and cancelled his ticket to Agra.

One extra week in Varanasi became four; one month stretched into five. He'd boated across the river nearly every day, bringing Vaman small bags of cooked rice and fruit, sticks of juniper incense for his shrine. Under the shade of an orange remnant of fabric, he and Vaman would talk on the sand for hours and then meditate until dusk.

Trepidatious at first, Sal began to join him for his morning baths in the river. Vaman taught him how to recite the holy mantras while submerging: *Asato ma sad gamaya. Lead me from ignorance to truth.* As the intensity of his fears and desires subsided, vibrations of bliss, deep and profound, began to form like ripples on the inner corridors of his being. The water became an icy, primordial cocoon that caressed every surface of his body. Low, tremoring, the sensations grew and then began to move him into waves of tears. All his silly aversions and unskillful words replayed so fiercely in his mind and then vanished for good. *Lead me from ignorance to truth.*

One afternoon, the turtle eggs began to hatch. Out on the promontory, dark circles emerged from the sand like oil slowly bubbling to the surface. With clumsy flippers the hatchlings struggled towards the river. Vaman pointed Sal's attention to the sky: A gyre of vultures spiraled lower. As others landed, the largest buzzard hopped to the nest with its collared neck and crooked wings at full extension. It stabbed its beak into the sand with a few swift pecks.

—*The turtles eat the bodies* - Vaman said.

—Bodies?

—*Of course* - he squinted across the Ganges at the columns of smoke lofting from the pyres - *After the dead are in the water, very soon, very soon they are gone. Some humans eat turtles, yes, but then some turtles eat humans, so I must ask myself every day, what will eat me? What can possibly do it! Brahma created the world and Shiva will destroy it. We must treasure these many aspects of God.*

Sal left the guesthouse with the TV behind him still broadcasting the disaster. He felt such unspeakable hatred at that wall of water, at its thunderous approach as it sped towards beaches spotted with curious families who had run out to the tide pools to gather shellfish. He wondered what it had all looked like from their perspective: Had they treasured God then? Had they praised their divine Creator as it roared at them with its velocity of barbarous indifference, a curled fist of ocean stretched so high it shadowed the sun? And for those who hadn't drowned, for those who'd clung to palm trees or held their breath, however they'd managed, everything had been lost or destroyed. Sometimes it was worse to survive a disaster. To survive meant you had to do something about it, to process the residue, to reconstruct a new philosophy from the rubble so as not to obliterate yourself in anger and hate.

Darkness in India no longer scared him. From the Rana ghat Sal walked along the labyrinth of steps and platforms until the Manikarnika ghat where cremations took place throughout the night. Still feared as cannibals, the Aghori sadhus sat by their fires in meditation. Sal carried nothing worth stealing, and the tsunami had confirmed to him that his life was as death-prone as anyone's. Once a protective shell, without his backpack he felt free and less vulnerable. Vaman had revealed to him his belongings had only been hindrances, a delusory coat of armour defending him against an already perfect reality he insisted on shying away from.

—*I am trying to serve Krishna with a pure heart* – Vaman admitted – *I am travelling for many many years, just observing, just looking, trying to understand. I leave everything, my home, my family, only to understand nature. Every way the human is searching. Everywhere, people are searching many things, but it is not so easy for us to find truth. You are living in five-stars, in air-conditioned rooms where everything is easy and perfect,*

17

and in this life we say we are searching for truth? What a funny world, Sal. A very funny world...

Vaman's fingers toyed with the string of beads he used to count his bhajans. He stood and looked at Sal without speaking, then squatted in the shallows of the river, splashing water over his arms. Farther down the bank, two boys kicked water at the pony; it backed away with small shifts of its hooves.

—What should I do? - Sal stepped into the water beside him.

—*That answer always depends on what you want to find.*

—You'll live on this sandbank forever? When the monsoon comes?

—*In the monsoon I will find new places to meditate. I no longer maintain illusions of permanence, Sal. I am not even convinced of being a sadhu forever. You see, I will die one day and so I will no longer be a sadhu. Only my skinny corpse will be a sadhu then!*

A charred leg shifted in the fire, paused, and then dropped out of the coals completely. Gripping it with tongs, an attendant placed it back on the pyre. Sal could see the skeletal mouth and gaping rows of teeth, the rib cage bowed like the curve of a hull. Its family stood throwing handfuls of marigolds onto the bed of embers. Here, the river was thick and sooty, and the water lapped up onto a small beach where the ashes and remnants were raked through and left for the waves. Sal pictured a phalanx of turtles drifting offshore just under the surface, their prehistoric eyes peering through waxy membranes for undevoured pieces. Everything seemed so potently clear when he observed the water closely.

Like Vaman said, death has been our destination from the beginning. It made sense when he'd heard it, but he'd never taken time to dwell on it. Standing here on the ghats as the sparks flew up towards the moon, he felt a peace settle into him. It would come. One day, maybe even tomorrow, his own extinguishment was sure to come. He'd given his backpack and shoes to the guesthouse owner. All that remained in his pockets were a few rupee notes and his ragged passport. They too were temporary, transient, uncertain. There was nothing in the world one could count on for stability. The disaster had proven that. Nature hadn't discriminated between good and evil, between tourists or locals. Death wouldn't either.

Instantly igniting, his passport flared into enlightened orange flames that cooled into ash. The fire attendant raked them against the shore where they hissed on the sand. Tonight Sal would sleep tucked into the stoop of some temple doorway, his body receiving with equanimity whatever sensations came and went. In the morning, he would boat across the Ganges to study alongside Vaman for good.

The sky had brightened to an early blue by the time the bow slid onto the sandbank. The melon farmers trimmed the vines with curved machetes, throwing the foliage into woven baskets strapped to their backs. A final spark of conviction shot through Sal. He was excited to tell Vaman what he'd done, the path he'd chosen. He wanted to see the young guru's eyes light up, to watch that grin crack beneath his beard. Life was uncertainty and Vaman had taught him to embrace its fluctuations without ever trying to manipulate them.

He arrived at the promontory and looked out at the ghats across the river half hidden in haze. So many ways to live, he thought. Yet underneath, one side or the other all the way down the Ganges to the Bay of Bengal, there was nothing but mud – thick with the sludge of old bones, crumbs from those turtles and the ashes of thousands – that even separated the two banks.

—*You are so pensive this day* – Vaman called from inside the shelter – *What have you been studying?*

—Waves. Bones. Catastrophes. Something happened in the ocean yesterday.

—*Yes, of course. Happenings as always.*

—Many people died. An earthquake and a massive wave.

Vaman crawled out of the hut, his hair matted and still dripping from his bath in the river.

—You were right. Nature is the best teacher of the human. You said that before.

—*The best teacher, yes, of how things truly are.*

Sal suddenly noticed Vaman's fire was a pit of cold ashes: He'd let it burn out. The stacks of cow manure were missing as well.

—I wanted to tell you – Sal continued – I made a commitment. I mean, that I'm serious about studying. I gave my things away. I burned my passport...

The sadhu squatted and began picking through the sand. He hadn't looked at Sal since he arrived. A surprise unease scratched at Sal's stomach.

—Is everything fine?

—*Yes, yes. Fine...yes, fine.*

—I'm telling you I came to study for good. I left everything.

—*That is good news, Sal. The life of a sadhu is difficult but rewarding. You will learn about a truth not many people know is even existing. I wish you luck and Krishna's fortune for this...but I must tell you. I have chosen to leave the sandbank.*

The young guru stood and gazed down the beach to the melon farmers and the boats arriving from across the river. He looked at the ghats and then down at Sal's feet.

—*As you know, I have lived here for many years as a sadhu. Every dry season I return and I have experienced much about the joy, the love, about what the human is searching for. But now I have a different curiosity.*

You see I put out my fire. I sold the dung for some rupees to take me to Varanasi. I don't know how I can do it, but I am curious to discover how humans live on that side. There must be a joy to have children, a family! To have a small room, to live with a wife and a grandmother. To spend the days working diligently as a chai walla or office man, there must be a joy in that too.

Sal felt the grains of sand burn into his soles. The haze had steamed off and a full Indian sun was beginning its temper.

—What kind of joy? - Sal countered - There's nothing over there. That's what I just realized, what you taught me. That's why I came here...

The city seemed like a giant wave perpetually cresting on the horizon, the colourful saris and longyis of the people like shattered debris lifting and churning in its momentum.

—*You are welcome to my hut* - Vaman stared at the ghats that lined the far bank - *It will last until the monsoon if you are lucky. Since I was a teenager, I have been only a sadhu. But I keep a curiosity about that shore I can no longer ignore. I need to participate in that fluxing, to share in that movement. Sure, to be a sadhu is easy. You don't have someone to say to you rules about waking, about clothings or behavior. We sadhus can be free as we like with no one but God to answer to. But there is no challenge to that life anymore. It feels so usual, so standard, so customary. Now I want to try and make the way of a life that will be a challenge to me. To help me grow, to use my practice for who needs it.*

In the laughter of the boys down the bank he heard the guesthouse owner in his dirty undershirt - *You'll be back* - Sal's stomach felt inflated by liquid.

—*I am happy you have decided to live in this way. It is a good way and you can learn very much. But I am so curious about this city I have watched from across the river day and night. Yes, I have been there before but as a sadhu, not a citizen. You too have this curiosity, Sal, so you can understand what it means to try.*

—Yes... – Sal paused. Except for a scalding breeze that hooked under the fabric of the hut and flapped it against the poles, there was a thick, oscillating silence – We should all try.

Vaman promised to visit the sandbank as soon as he could. Sal watched him wade down the beach to a boat and the boat was pushed off the sand by the boy holding the reins of the pony. *Think you the first white man to come to India and meet a guru?* A vapor of sadness collected on the insides of his breath. He pictured the fishing villages on the southern coast, Sri Lanka, the beaches of Thailand full of inquisitive tourists camcording the wave as it grew and towered above them and then swept them away. He saw the surface of the Ganges roil as the turtles snapped hold of an arm bone or pelvis, shredding it of its meat. He watched Vaman's boat disappear into the chaos of the far shore. In one month, the monsoons would arrive on the horizon, a banister of cloud that would send Sal eastward towards the ocean.

THE PIGEONS OF PESHAWAR

Men wrapped in shawls weave bicycles through oncoming streams of rickshaws. Two-pitched car horns startle the spit from mules. Wagons of bricks rumble past, emphatic and wrestling along the road's pocked pavement. Gathered at their motorbikes, gangs of Sikh men yawn and toy beneath their fingernails, awakening in the diesel-fumed dawn. Against the wall of Lahore station – a lingering sand-brick fortress of British Imperialism parked on Pakistan's eastern border with India – the roadside swells in front of my plastic stool as the barber leans in. From the mosque's turret, a black compass point against the haze of the Punjabi plains, the muezzin sirens out the call to prayer: The holy moans of Islam coat the waking city.

—No turning – his chestnut hand steadies my brow – You want to save your head? Still, still.

As his razor scrapes my jaw, the cologne of his wrist lands in my nostrils – spiced aftershave mixed with the sweat of his undershirt. His eyes are yellowed, their corners faintly blood-shot; his ebony moustache is coarse and blunt as a broom. Leaning to the barbers next to him, he exhibits the blade he's drawn. Men in coloured shalwars peer in from behind: Semi-circular, hands hooked, they are curious and indolent at the sight of me, my whiskers, the strangeness of my downhill skis propped against the station's wall. Their notes of Urdu laugh-ter perch on my shoulders as they study the blond stubble litter-ing the heap of foam.

—Gold beard – he wipes the razor on a scrap of cloth and brings it again to my lip.

Here is that alien bewilderment, that deeper paralysis of difference. Here the history fields still vibrate in their aftermath like the heartbeat of a bomb. It is right to have come, I affirm, wading through this strangeness alone while Adrian is still far-ther, still ahead of me, settled in a guesthouse somewhere high in the Karakoram. We are ten years older and have let the drift of our lives separate us like an ice floe. Our purpose for coming, we reasoned and planned weeks earlier via email, was that once on our skis again, we might finally outrun what had chased us since high school.

—Finished – the barber blots me with a corner of newsprint – Beautiful as a boy.

—*Shukria* – I say. Thank you.

—You are leaving Lahore? – he inquires – Today? So soon?

—This evening's train. Lahore to Islamabad and then Gilgit to Karakoram.

—Gilgit? – he worries his eyebrows – *Inshallah*, you will be safe. They are proud to be bandits there. Lacking shame! Some birds eat fruit and other birds eat flesh. I pray you encounter only those with beaks made for berries.

—*Inshallah* – I hand him a five-rupee note, take my skis and pass between the stares of the shalwar men back into the flutter of the station.

The interior hall is a carnival of travellers, the Pakistani railways churning at full throttle. Turbaned porters ferry sacks of onions and firewood, ticket vendors holler their destinations from speakers wired near the ceiling fans. Like a belt, this station is Pakistan's buckle to the subcontinent, a suture to the severed shore of the Indian wound.

After an overnight train from Delhi I arrived in Lahore before dawn. Crossing the border in the dark, my carriage was a party of celebrating Sikh pilgrims. I couldn't sleep for the heat and noise so I lay on the mid-tier bunk, rocking, staring out the window at the passing countryside. Moonlit palm trees laid indigo shadows onto the fields. The unfamiliar constellations of this hemisphere rotated in the black sky beyond them. I watched as a man on horseback galloped beside the train, the moonlight carving between the animal's hooves as it ran. I could have sworn the rider caught my eye and grinned as he rode, his teeth gleaming in the milky light. Hunched forward, he galloped faster. I felt drenched in the adrenaline of far, of utter distance, as though I had reached the foggiest corner of the planet that still held some perfect secret, where it was all sights and sounds altered from what I knew or could imagine.

Here, the unparallel life-fringed border to the ribbon of travel – roadsides, tracksides, hillsides, waysides. The world, I assure myself, is full of birds that eat berries.

Adrian and I had arranged for our guide to the glacier, a local man named Akram, to meet my train, and although there'd been an email from him the previous day confirming my arrival, he hadn't been at the station like he promised. Without a way to get in contact, I resigned to wait out the day alone. I found a cart selling naan and dhal and then paid for a shave with the roadside barber. Now against the wall of the central platform as the sun transforms the city from indigo to orange, I find a clean-swept corner to lay my backpack and skis and wait for him. I'll watch for him here and if he never shows, I'll take the train to Islamabad myself. After ten years, face to face with Adrian tonight, I have imagined shaking his hand a thousand times. Adrian, who had frozen some object inside me that had broken off and begun travelling my coasts like an iceberg.

DHUHR – 11:52 AM

—Shane, buddy! – Adrian's webcam image stammered in low-res with the poor connection. Behind him the streets of Islamabad ignited my laptop's screen – Are you really coming?

—Got the skis waxed already.

—Man, you've never seen anything like this place. It's something real, that's for sure.

—I think I just saw a herd of goats pass behind you. Yeah, I'm coming. Of course I am. You sure those hills are worth the trip?

—Hills? My God, Shane, these aren't hills. They're goddamn monsters. But we're skiing glaciers this time. Biafo, right? She's got K2 in the background and the largest run of pristine snow outside the poles. You up for it? I know you remember some of the tricks I taught you in practice. Monsters, buddy. Nasty goddamn ghouls.

The Biafo Glacier, a powder-topped tongue of frozen till edged by mile-deep crevasses. Tucked in a forsaken notch of Pakistan, the glacier creeps between the Karakoram, the icy foothills of the Himalayas, inch by inch toward the ocean.

—You sure you can make it here alone? I've told the guys all about you and our crazy times on ski team. Did you know no one else keeps in touch with their mates from high school? Is that weird or what?

—I'll be coming a few weeks early to see the sights in Delhi so I'll meet you in Gilgit.

—Man, this place is the real deal, I'm telling you. Those runs we did for team were a driveway compared to these.

The image of Adrian turned in a sweep of pixels as a group of women clad in burkas entered the café behind him, their curtains of fabric disguising them like bandits caught on security camera.

—Those the goats you were talking about? - Adrian turned back to the screen, all teeth in the webcam - I'm telling you, Shane, it's the dark side of the moon here. You'll love it. I'll send Akram to meet you wherever you want. Lahore's a fun town. Take the train from Delhi and meet him there. He's the son of two rich Pakis but British as they come. You'll see, Shane, he's hysterical.

—It'll be great to see you.

—No kidding, buddy. Ten years go by in a flash.

Ten years since high school, since the ski team with Adrian when we rode to the top of the slope together, our feet dangling above the tree caps. From the chair behind us Mr. Mason called out – *Boys, I want to see you work the fall line directly as possible. Got it? Carve tight off the front trough while keeping your pace constant.* Adrian always gunned out the deepest moguls with reckless speed. His knees sprung to his chest like bullets, his boots held tight together and with the biggest, boyish grin washing over his face as he flew the jumps in twisters and spread eagles. He could land solidly, purposefully, with all the confidence of an athlete who knew how to make winning look easy. Propped on his poles at the bottom of the run, he stared up at me, his braces glinting through his smile. *Come on, Shane!* – he called – *Hit it dead centre and you'll fly when you hit the lip!* I envied him then, I remember, envied those braces even, linking his teeth like miniature scaffolds. How he knew he had the talent so couldn't give a fuck about anything else.

Somewhere down the platform, shouts emerge from an administration office. The static of radios crackles the heat as a squadron of officers pushes from the far end through groups of lingering travellers. The brass details on their military insignia flash as they cut through slats of sunlight angled from the ventilation shafts. As they vanish into the room, drafts of pigeons suddenly loose from the rafters and flap across the stone canopy, arching as one body into a frantic grey landing – a chorus of warbles pecking crumbs from the ochre tile. Squatting at the wall, a toothless woman fans a pot of curry she balances on a charcoal tin. She nods at me, opens her cruddy gums and heaves a laugh in my direction, bringing her hands to her sides in the shape of two gnarled wings. She flaps and laughs again.

More shouts as the crowd outside the office grows, each man craning to see inside. Curious, I stand, walk down the platform and join the peering men. On the administrator's desk inside the room sits a small television, its wire antennae kinked and taped to the plaster wall. The screen flickers a newscast of a street scene deep in Pakistan – the grime-caked city of Peshawar. The crowd jostles its heat around me, a human herd damp with beards and turbans, ciphers of Urdu, Pashto and Punjabi. I glance back at my skis left propped against the wall. Strange to see them meet this foreignness, so far from their mountains, so far from where they'd lain for ten years in my garage next to garden hoses, bags of birdseed, rakes and bicycles.

A voice calls out behind me – You are going to Peshawar? You must alter your plans if you are.

When I turn I meet the face of a young man, brown and boyish-skinned. Black hair sweeps across his forehead; he is dressed in an olive-green shalwar with eyes the clear tourmaline of glaciers. His black lashes draw out a hint of moustache.

—I would not go to Peshawar if I were you – he continues – Not today.

—Islamabad, but not until this evening. What happened there?

He pushes in front of a row of grey-bearded men and stands next to me – The Taliban made an assault. A prison has been attacked and they have freed nearly four hundred convicts. I am afraid now Pakistan is very dangerous for you. They will cancel the train to Peshawar until more notice.

—And for Islamabad?

—Wait, wait. I will ask – he presses through to the window. After a jabber of Urdu, the office attendant nods his head, waving him away disinterestedly.

The boy pushes back to me – There is still a train to Islamabad. This evening, yes.

—Good – I extend him my hand – That's good. I'm Shane.

—Sahir. And from Islamabad, where will you go?

—Gilgit and the Karakoram.

—I knew it. The mountains – Sahir's face frees into a smile. Like the son of some Kashmiri diplomat with high Zoroastrian cheekbones, his teeth are starched, untarnished, shockingly aligned. A descendent of handsome, high-nosed Greeks left in his bloodline from Alexander the Great, he stands like a vintage postcard against the backdrop of the station – They are beautiful, that is what I hear.

—It's why I came.

—We in Pakistan are very proud of our country. More so, we are proud of the foreigners who dare to come here. But you are alone and there are serious dangers for people of your flesh tone. Your skin is more valuable to some than a tiger's.

—Everyone prefers to dress themselves in the hides of other animals. My friend Akram, he's late. He's taking me to Islamabad this evening.

—Then you have time for a tour of Lahore station – Sahir brightens – I'm sure you must be curious about many things in our history. As my father tells me, it is peace for the soul to revisit the cages of our past as different men.

ASR – 2:40 PM

It was nearing the end of first term when the smell of winter hit the air. Something metallic, zinc or nickel, signalled the snow was about to fall. While everyone else dreaded the approaching cold, Adrian and I plotted the length of the coming ski season, how many weekends still ahead, how many runs. We sketched out the tricks we wanted to master in elaborate coloured diagrams. It felt good to embrace what others wouldn't, to love something others rejected.

The bright fluorescents of the hallway stoked the red lockers as Adrian came up to me, pulling me into the empty computer lab.

—Check this out – he grinned in the darkness – Guess who.

His phone's screen had a series of messages from a number I didn't recognize.

—*Looking forward to the season?*

—*Sure. I'm keen to try the 360.*

—*360's for big boys. Got an extra pair of those boxers you wear?*

—*Dozens. Why? They're Costco. U want some?*

—*I meant for the 360. But you offering?*

—*Got some old pairs. Yours if you want them.*

—*My kind of guy. Send a pic in them first if you're up for it.*

The force of my heart swallowed my eardrums; something sour, thick and unquenchable sucked the moisture off my tongue.

—Mr. Mason?

—Yep.

—Holy shit...

—Got a bunch more like these. Creepy, huh?

—Yeah, for sure. Creepy.

I felt kinked in the thorax, that place where on an insect its thinness is so frightening you fear its body will snap in two. The light from Adrian's phone caught his braces like a diamond mine. I wanted braces more than ever after that, I remember. I caressed the invisible cores of metal I longed to be cemented to my teeth. Calcium, frostbit aluminum, the galvanized steel poles of a schoolyard fence I'd once pressed my tongue to on a dare. The yank of pink flesh, the frostbitten drool of panic, a pale, glacier-hued odour of snow.

—But who cares anyway. He's a perv, so what's the harm, right? – Adrian bit the phone, exposing his teeth – He's pushing me hard this season and I need him to get me ready for

Junior's. Turin is in five years. What do you think, can you believe it? Mason is friends with the coach of the Canadian team. You know what it would mean to make the Olympics? I've got a shot at it, you know that, right?

—Don't say anything – I prayed my breath hadn't quickened – Not to anyone.

▲ ▲ ▲

Sahir leads me from the departure platform to the main hall teeming with passengers, his hand outstretched behind him – Come, come. I will show you something you cannot see in palaces. This way, Shane.

My skis are hoisted on my shoulder; my duffel bag packed with snow gear hangs from me like a harness. Rivulets of heat breach the back of my shirt. We cross through a series of anterooms stocked with bundles and parcels in knotted fabric, torn-taped, walling in clans of seated women in shalwars of purple, tangerine and emerald, obliterating themselves with jewelled dupatta scarves.

—We still have many problems since partition – Sahir says – When we Muslims left India we gave our hearts to Lahore. Even then, as symbolic as this city is, it too has seen its share of violence – he points at the floor for emphasis – There have been bombs, explosions, here in this station.

—When the Muslims left India?

—Bodies clogged the aisles, under the seats, even filling the lavatories. When the Bombay Express arrived here, no person remained alive except one. One survivor of two thousand – the engineer, an Englishman. The Sikhs from Bhatinda massacred them. Do you know what it means to give your heart to something others want dead?

—You have beautiful areas too – I say – The Himalayas, Biafo, the Karakoram. That's where I'm going to ski.

—There are many mountains here, but not many who are fortunate enough to be skiers. Leave your things in this office. I will show you something special from this sweltering cage I am kept in.

Sahir turns down a corridor to a musty room where a turbaned man squats amid stacks of baggage reading a newspaper – He is my friend, don't worry. He will watch your things for no charge while we finish the tour, yes?

Without my bags, the cool of the midday breeze hits the damp of my shirt. I feel the lightness that comes from having set down the heaviest loads, the freedom of moving forward unencumbered.

Outside the rear of the station, we stand on an abandoned platform of cracked asphalt. Leggy weeds flower in the baking sun; pigeons warble somewhere in the eaves. Steel tracks wander the yard unused like the ruts of forgotten wagons. There is a quiet here that feels almost rural. I look out at the yard's fence line, to the clusters of soot-caked buildings and edifices of peeling advertisements for Punjabi action films and soda brands. Hitched to an orange cart, the semitonal haw of a donkey tumbles the fence from a side street. From beneath the haze emerge the spired domes and sunburnt turrets of the Emperor's

Mosque, the low wail of the noontime call to prayer. Farther still in the distant hills, those prisoners of Peshawar running free. What trains were pulled along these tracks, I think. What massacred people?

—Come this way – Sahir jumps onto the gravel hugging the rail ties so solid and brimful with history – Quickly, Shane. This way!

To our right, a row of carriages pulls from the station; an engine chugs and draws, heaving its massive weight forward. As it accelerates, a line of men sprints beside it, grabbing onto the handholds, leaping up and inside. One after the other as the train speeds up, the men are pulled up to the roof by the hands of those crouching on top, their shalwars flapping in the breeze.

—We men love to take chances, don't we? – Sahir looks back at me – You must take risks to feel the full rewards of freedom, don't you agree?

He flashes a grin, startling and familiar. Behind him, the train capped with turbaned men disappears into the hot smog of Lahore.

MAGHRIB – 4:59 PM

I remember that feeling of relief when Mr. Mason's texts began arriving to my phone as well. He had the numbers of all the skiers on the team to reach us in case we lost track of time or wandered off-piste, to rein in an energetic flock of boys released across the mountainside. Relief, I remember, galvanized into a kind of pride I could only share with Adrian. I remember walking through the hallways, taller, dragging my hand along the lockers, trying to suppress a grin.

—*Nice practice today. Feeling more confident?*

—*Yeah, felt like I improved my approach a lot.*

—*You're not as brave as the others. You play it safe. It shows in your speed.*

—*I like to know what I'm doing before I try a new trick. Speed's fine, I guess.*

—*Risk isn't for everyone. We'll have to loosen you up next time.*

—*Yeah, I could use that. I tighten up when I'm nervous.*

—*Bet you're tight a lot of places* :)

Something drew down in Adrian's face as he read, the muscles around his lips tightening into the flexes of a scowl.

—You ever send him that picture? – I asked – I'm thinking I should send him one too.

—It's true – Adrian stepped back, suddenly bolder – You don't take enough chances. That's what makes you such a lousy skier anyways. If it were up to you, you'd just follow in my tracks the whole way down.

—What? No way.

—You can't even do a simple spread eagle. And the whole team has to baby you on a twist.

—Fine, I won't take one. Who even cares?

That night at practice the snow was ice crystals and pellets; they shot through the air like artillery, soaked our jackets and formed a stubborn drag our skis resisted. I didn't ride the lift with Adrian. I watched him a few chairs ahead scraping at the slush on his ski with his pole, the slope's lights dim aureoles behind the blizzard. Later, I looked down to see Mr. Mason coaching Adrian at the kicker. I felt sick, snapped in two, when Adrian launched into the air, spun and landed a 360. I watched Mr. Mason ski down and shake him by his shoulders, cheering. The snow's wetness permeated my gloves, my jacket, my hoodie, my T-shirt to my skin, the chairlift carrying me deeper into the clouds.

Two weeks later, Adrian found me by my locker. His eyes were red with the remnants of tears he'd wiped away quickly, his posture a strange blend of the macho I admired him for and the skulking of a scraped-kneed boy.

—I'm off the team – his lashes were damp clumps – Fuck those motherfuckers. Suspended too.

—What do you mean? Who?

—Mr. Mason and Mr. Lucas. I just had a meeting in the principal's office. All three called me in. Cocksuckers kicked me off the team.

—What? What for?

—It was just an old roach, not even a joint. Mr. Lucas caught me behind the portable yesterday. He took me to the office right away, stoned as hell – he rubbed his thumb along the metal edge of my open locker – You've got to help me, Shane. I'm a dick for saying you were a shit skier, but you've got to help me. I'm not giving up Turin for one lousy roach – he sniffed; it sounded like he loaded a rifle – Did you save those messages? The ones from Mr. Mason?

I remember the hallway turning dark and tubular, red as guts, the doorway at the end a far and unreachable galaxy. In my ears I heard the ski lift ratcheting us up to a peak we'd never skied or ever dared to.

It was the right thing to do, to help Adrian, I persuaded myself, though for nights I didn't sleep or slept fitfully, waking in tangled intervals embroidered with craving and dread. Success begs to be shared, I reasoned, so we should abandon our fear, we should face the enemy. Square and emboldened, I grew to want Turin for Adrian as much as he did. I fortified his plan because I feared losing him from the team, feared holding a secret I couldn't share with anyone if he left. We agreed to show the messages to our parents, to allow them to contact school authorities, to confront Mr. Mason together.

Still, in memory, those days are a collection of images edited together like old camcorder video. The way my mother's fork touched her plate as it trembled, how she left the pots in the sink and went to bed early. How in the meeting Mr. Mason was stone-faced and I searched him for fissures of anger, betrayal, hurt, but found none. Pillared between our parents, we shielded our phones in our palms, charged and sweaty with evidence. How Adrian was asked to load his photographs onto a laptop, to stand squinting beneath the alien light of the projector as it cast a pale image of his bony torso in boxer shorts onto the chalkboard. How I was asked to stand and do the same for the images on mine. Both of us were silent, teary-eyed travellers in confrontation with a part of the world we'd dropped ourselves into yet couldn't comprehend, a planet abuzz with such strangeness it paralyzed us to the bone. How the principal's voice crumbled the air at last saying, *That's fine now, boys. That will do.* How the clock above us froze in the fluorescents, how the texture of shame knotted the carpets, the chalk dust, the sound of handcuffs clicking shut. How neither of us could lift ourselves to look as the policemen led Mr. Mason from the room. How the red rotation of the cruiser's lights flashed off the classroom's unfamiliar surfaces. How the guilt of a consequence could be so much worse than the crime.

Adrian and I were asked to be present for the arraignment hearing. The list of charges looped in my head like the coaching mantras I replayed before a downhill run: *Luring and invitation to sexual touching involving minors. Commission and possession of child pornography.*

—You sent him those kinds of photos? – I whispered.

Adrian toyed with the end of his tie – Who cares?

A strange expression played around his face and it took me a moment to notice. He looked over at me and smiled without smiling, running his tongue across his teeth, newly smooth, porcelain-straight.

—Holy shit – I whispered.

Mr. Mason pled not guilty and posted his bail.

ISHA – 6:25 PM

—The most special thing about Pakistan is that we men are free to do as we please – Sahir lights a cigarette and kicks an empty bottle through the stalky weeds in the gravel – Do you smoke?

—No, thank you.

—We rule the land as birds over a valley. We are free to jump onto the tracks, to chase whatever train we wish to catch. Do you see what I mean?

—That's why I ski, to find a piece of that feeling – I answer. A feeling like I've left the earth for a moment, flown, gained a softer perspective of snow and ice and blazing altitude, to subdue something powerful, force it into forgiving me.

—I have always wished to ski – Sahir says – Yet that is dangerous too. A few days ago in Kashmir an avalanche swallowed nearly two hundred soldiers. They ski down the glaciers from post to post with their rifles, the highest military base in the world. Do you believe that? Guarding the mountains as if someone would steal them.

—Dangerous – I say – There is nowhere safe in the universe.

With his cigarette Sahir gestures out at the reddish haze above the city, the vibrations of the muezzin's calls crippling the dusk – May I ask why you came here? Why Pakistan?

Clouds of crystalline powder shower the slope as the metal edges of our skis shave the alpine skin to blue flesh. Utter wilderness and exhilaration, to explore the exploded heartbeat instead of fleeing from it. To find freedom from gravity, from consequences. Although a decade ago, I want Adrian to know that when the news came on, Mr. Mason's face was a cyan-magenta-yellow rendering above the text: ACCUSED TEACHER KILLED BY TRAIN, LAYS HIMSELF ON TRACKS DAYS

BEFORE TRIAL. That I cried for us all as I read and vomited until I was hoarse. That I lay at the toilet's pedestal, heaving and exhausted, that I ran my astringent tongue across my teeth and thought of him. That I nurtured no resentment, no envy, when years later I heard he'd made the team for Turin. That I wheeled a friend's television seven blocks in a shopping cart to the house where I boarded in college to watch his qualifying round. That I gasped when I saw his skis contact ice and his legs fly out from under him and his body flail above the rippled braid of mounded snow, an impossible matrix of limbs and poles and catastrophe. That I felt it all for him as if it had been me.

—Have you ever heard of ghosts? They're thin and white and made of air. They follow you to the ends of the earth crying out for things you can't give. I thought they couldn't follow me here but they did.

—They will only leave you in peace once you submit – the blue of Sahir's eyes is clear as an iceberg – Yes, ghosts. We in Pakistan know them well but it is in both of our interests that we learn to coexist. We must strive to become better men, no matter the cage of our past. What is wrong? You look as though your mule has run. Are you sad for something?

—No – I say – Just done, just through with phantoms. Tired and anxious. I want to ski.

—Your train too – Sahir says, standing – We must begin looking for your friend.

The departure hall seems aged ten years. Families sprawl asleep amid the baggage; swarms of insects tick against the ceiling fans, their husks piling the corners of the floor in drifts. Re-entering the station, I breathe in that same feeling I had when stranded at school late at night after practice. Something dark and empty coated the familiar corridors yet made them seem kinder, less school somehow, more sanctuary. I try to picture Sahir's boyhood days, the classrooms he studied and recited in, the moths that flicked along the sills as he chanted the Koran or memorized the dates of old massacres, the ghosts of his country stalking the land beyond the window.

—You see, your things are safe – Sahir leads me into the baggage room. My skis and duffel bag are propped in the corner, dim relics in a museum archive – If you like, I will carry them for you. Don't worry, I don't ask that you pay me, this is my pleasure.

Sahir runs his hands over the lacquered finish of the planks, reading the binding mechanism, thumbing the edges' razor.

—And in here? – he weighs the duffel.

—The boots. They're heavy. I'll take them.

He ignores me, hooking the straps over one shoulder. He tucks the skis beneath his arm, his grin the widest Cheshire – It really is my pleasure.

When we approach the main hall, Akram is propped against the wall staring at the platform congested with pigeons. Small and agile, he looks like a bespectacled tour guide in charge of an unruly gaggle of kids. He exhales when he sees me, comes to his feet and opens his arms for a hug.

—Oh, my God, Shane. Can you believe this country? – his arms pull tight around me – We're supposed to be glad the

British left but I can't see a single redeeming benefit if the trains don't run on time.

—It's good you're here. I spent the day with Sahir.

Sahir stands at my side holding the skis, the duffel bag, looking on as though trying to decipher a code.

—*Assalaamu alaykum* – Akram gestures to him – But it's not fine, Shane. My train was supposed to arrive eight hours ago. You've been waiting all day and I'm afraid it's all for nothing. We can't even go to Islamabad.

—What? What for?

—The expedition's been cancelled. That bloody prison break, didn't you hear? The Taliban has freed the lot of them, terrorists and kidnappers, isn't that right? The Consulate wants us out. Too dangerous, they say. Well how bloody dangerous is a glacier anyway? You won't find Al-Qaeda on skis, will you? I'm sorry you came all this way, but it's finished. Awful, I know.

—Finished? That's it?

—Adrian's fuming. You can't imagine how livid he is. The poor man is convinced he'll never get to ski another day in his life. I don't blame him. But thank God you came when you did. This train is the Samjhauta leaving for Attari. We'll be back to civilization in under an hour if we can catch it. What a hellhole. We'd have been better off in Nepal despite the Maoists. Come, I've already bought you a ticket.

The departure hall reverberates with the announcer's voice amplified off the heat and stone. Carriages creak and snap at their hitches, their wheels popping free of inertia as the train begins to roll.

—Come on, Shane. It would crush me to have to spend the night here.

Sahir jogs with me beside the doors of the moving carriage, the skis and duffel bag large and unwieldy.

—You jump inside – he says – I will pass them to you. Go now. You see it's speeding up.

Running with the carriage, the train accelerates as Akram leaps aboard. I grab hold of the bar beside the door, jump and pull myself up and inside.

—Your skis first... – Sahir shouts, running.

—Keep them – I say – They're yours.

The steady clack of rails, its rocking speed, the sudden end of the asphalt platform like a precipice leapt and flown from. Sahir comes to a standstill, his green shalwar looped in the straps of my bags as we pull away into the cinder-bricked suburbs of Lahore graffitied by curls of Urdu script. Back to India, I think, to the safety of borders.

—You're as good as a pro – Akram says as we catch our breaths – Few Indians will even play at that game, and even then only the crazy ones. But Shane, why did you give him those skis? That boy won't be able to use them in a thousand years.

—To give him something to flee with – I think – To save himself, to outrun avalanches.

—Thank God we didn't have to spend the night. A bloody hellhole, I tell you.

A train rumbles and sways in the kind of cadence the body remembers. In the seats ahead, the saris of women ripple in the evening breeze. Akram's head tilts to his chest in a doze. Already I feel the new growth of stubble roughen my chin, the border of India fifty kilometres ahead in the dusk, the passing farmland statued with goats and waddles of geese being led to their grassy creeks by shepherds in white turbans.

I wake in the night as the train suddenly slows. We crawl forward in approach to a crowd, a hundred men, semi-circular, crammed tight to the tracks. The sea of their faces passes my window near enough I smell the heat off their skin. In the mass of them, I swear I see one with the face of Mr. Mason, cold-eyed, acquitting, the whites of his irises flashing at me beneath police lights. There is the flapping of furious wings against my stomach, a whole flock panicking as one bird falls in a spray of feathers, hooked by the predator's claws. Through a break in the crowd, there is a dune of cloth and severed flesh, the dusty heap of a man on the tracks, his shalwar soaked in red, the skin of his feet, still in sandals, turned grey.

LES 3 CHEVALIERS

Our motorcycle pulls up in front of the bar; its red sign reflects in the puddles below the crumbling sidewalk. We step and scatter the red into ripples. The night air settles wet over our surfaces.

—Yeah? On my life, you like this bar! – Piat, wide-grinned, leans the bike on its stand, twirls keys on his fingers – You come in! Come this bar, I show you girls. You see if you like, and if you no like, you no buy.

Wet season. Rain clouds hover on the horizon until four o'clock and as the sun descends, they scuttle over the city and wring themselves out in short bursts. Emerging into the clear air beneath, the sun licks an orange tongue over their bottom surfaces and turns the shivering reflection of the lake into a pit bright as magma. Travellers gather on the wooden porches of the surrounding guesthouses snapping photos in pleasant disbelief Phnom Penh has turned out to be so beautiful. Water hyacinths drift in clumps. Hammocks creak their sway along the beams. Piat wanders from table to table selling bags of skunk weed and Zippo lighter knock-offs. When someone asks about the corrupt government or how's life in Cambodia today for a boy of eighteen, he cries – It not good! On my life, it not good!

The Killing Fields is on for the third time in the background. Shlomi looks over his shoulder at the TV then lays his head on his arms on the table.

I say – Fuck, that joint did me in too. What's it like in Israel anyway? Ever shoot a man with your gun? – and then stub the roach out in the plastic lid of the water bottle.

—Never killed a man.

Israelis. I've always wanted to get to know one of them but they've always been ones to dance off to the side of things, cigarettes propped in tanned faces, shirtless, shooting pool with the newly arrived Swedish girls. They carry themselves proud like the French, still with their army dog-tags, whiffs of arrogance and stick-together. Whole guesthouses in Bangkok just for Israelis. But this one broke off the pack. He stood next to my table, looked down into my milkshake and said – What is that? Coconut?

—Banana.

—It doesn't look yellow to me – he'd lifted his chin with Israeli smugness.

—Never killed a man – baked and bleary-eyed, he lifts his head from his arms – We weren't there to kill them, just to make them uncomfortable, you know. Just to keep them on edge. We were trained not to admit weakness to the enemy. So what if we make them wait five or six hours at checkpoints? So what if they have to line up for gasoline? It lets them know we're not kidding. That's our job. We fuck up their lives a bit. They wait because they have to, and we make them wait because we have to. It's all just a bunch of kids in uniforms anyway...

—For no reason?

—Of course there's a reason. Do you know what it takes just to keep a war going? Year after year with all the soldiers in their uniforms, the complexity of that machine? You know they invented bullets that change directions in your body? It goes in your shoulder, fucks up your bones, fucks up your organs then leaves through your leg. What do you think that shit costs?

Smoke ponders the space above the table.

—Do you know what a bullet costs?

—I've got a right to go wherever I like in this sad little country... – From the bar, Khoi stares across the room at the TV with indifferent noontime eyes.

—*I've got a right to go wherever I like in this sad little country!* – Sam Waterston's voice shouts from the speakers under chopper blades – *That's their law. That's our law.*

—...up the Cooper-Church Amendment's ass...

—*Well, up the Cooper-Church Amendment's ass!*

Khoi looks over at us – Sure, I know this movie. One hundred thousand times I see this movie. Every time new people come to this guesthouse they want to see *Killing Fields*. Maybe one million times I see this movie!

Shlomi says – These your cigarettes?

—Every time. Every time they want *Killing Fields*. Hey, you have an iPod?

Khoi and I sit on the wooden deck built out over the water. Sparse lights dot the opposite shore like a band of constellations. Somewhere on the lake a motor throbs through the hyacinths, its wake knocking them against the posts of the deck. In the dark their surface looks solid enough to stand on.

—As boys, we ride on the back of the buffalo and they take us through the rice – he says – Yeah, really! They don't care. You just sit on their back and they walk around the fields and eat grass. In the monsoon we go into the rice and look for snake, you know, because snake don't like water and so they are more easy to catch. Even when we have nothing to do, my brothers and sisters we play and we walk outside and make games. That is life here. Yeah. Now Cambodia have many problem. But before, Cambodia have *big* problem.

Piat tosses words with a man swinging in the hammock beside the entrance of the bar. With a chewed toothpick he pries into the crusts of his knuckles. Two girls with bare midriffs play with their nails on blue stools along the wall. A curtain of red beads is pinned back from the doorway.

—He ask if you have weapon.

—No weapons.

The bar is humid and foul-smelling inside. The walls are black and coated in red light from the bulbs in the low ceiling. At one end, a small platform supported by crates serves as a stage. Three girls are inside – one in the corner, one behind the bar, one just disappeared into a back room with her arm around a shirtless man. The girl's face at the bar is familiar as all of Southeast Asia. Red lips, a low nose with a flat bridge and flared nostrils. She has a patina to her skin that reveals exposure to heavier atmospheres, to particles of history that have burrowed into her irises, lined her face, accumulated beneath her lacquered fingernails like someone who has pawed at the earth for a reason.

—Hi, handsome, what you want for tonight? You stay with me? What you like? - Thick as honey, her dripping voice. She chatters to the girl from the corner with the bigger nose, rolls of brown fat, a bad haircut. The uglier one who takes the sadder jobs.

Piat orders whiskey and flips through a binder of CDs.

—She speak English. Tell her what you want.

What I want. What is that thing anyway? A trail of inflammations the bedbugs left from a dirty mattress in Bangkok I want to X through with my fingernail? Want. The shade of damp marijuana, a fishing net anchored by hyacinth roots? *That's their law. That's our law.* Ass. Firm brown nipples rubbed against sheer. Want is an imagined future harvested from lake bottoms of bones. At the door, an argument happens in sign language: two deaf lesbians.

Black storm clouds hover in the west over the lake. Two boys fish in a canoe using nets they lay and pull back in. Shlomi spies on them with the binoculars and says - Every day for hours and hours. What will they do when it starts to rain?

—Cover their heads and paddle to shore. Our definitions of risk are different. They ride six to a bike here.

Piat strolls into the guesthouse with deliberate footsteps, his keys twirling. Wild eyes, high, sunken cheekbones, gestures he throws beyond his body limits into the surrounding air – On my life, man! You still here? I come from the market, you know, I meet my honey, eat noodles. You want to buy some skunk?

A recovering glue sniffer, a street kid who's found a profession, he must be. His face doesn't twitch but stretches into the most crazed and opened expressions. His laughs string enormous bridges of saliva across the corners of his lips. Selling skunk to stoner backpackers earns him a few thousand riel to buy noodles for his girlfriend at the market and a few tabs of M. He'll take you on his motorbike to Choeung Ek and wait around as you tour the fields and collect souvenir photos in high-def – skulls towered in pyramids, thigh bones stacked like timber, torn fabric still sprouting from the soil. Just like in the movie. Ten thousand riel for the day, S-21 prison included – *Before, Cambodia no good, you know?* – Isn't that what I want to hear?

Beside the bar, the blackboard reads: *Tonight – Killing Fields 7 pm.* Ceiling fans whirl and scatter threads of smoke unravelled from hands in sagging hammocks. A few travellers eating eggs watch CNN, compare the routes they took to Angkor, how much they enjoyed Laos. Beyond the deck, the morning sun has not yet risen into the bank of grey clouds.

I say to Piat – Where you been? Stay out all night?

Laughing, wild eyes with morning hair – No, man, I get this! Fresh today, you see? Best weed grows in Battambang, but in Phnom Penh you can only buy from me. No buy in Siem Reap or Sihanoukville. If you want, buy now. Later, I don't have, you know. I smoke too much!

—I dunno...

—Why not! Come on, man, just buy my skunk!

A little weed for the coming weather isn't such a bad idea. The guy's price is high, but he's so damn charming I feel I owe him the business.

—I'll buy skunk and you take me to S-21 prison today for free.

His mouth stretches open in a huge gulp of laughter, his eyes disappear and those constant tendons of drool – Free? Come on, man! Now gasoline is very high price! Now Cambodia no good! Skunk already good price, you know, friend price. On my life! How much you pay?

Bag of skunk, Tuol Sleng prison, and tonight a trip to his favorite girlie bar – only couple thousand riel. But if he's happy with it, I know I've gotten screwed. Here it's always this push–pull: Don't rip or get ripped off. Cheap Charlie peeling bills from a sweaty money-belt, his peripheral vision on vigilant lookout for thieves. The sucker white guy with bottomless pockets of dollars.

Piat pitches his skunk deal to an Australian in a hammock. The Israeli walks across the deck over to my table, looks down at my milkshake and says – What is that, coconut?

Girl with the flat nose shouts over to Piat and their thick Khmer tumbles over the bar. He hands her a CD to put into the portable stereo in the corner on the floor by the stage. She bends over, a hole yawning open in her stockings – the upper thigh near the crease of her ass. Cambodian rap punches through shitty speakers. The lesbians sit brooding on the bar stools in silence. The two girls from outside sidle up to us.

Piat says – See look, my honeys!

The wide-nosed girl says – What you like, handsome? You want to see my menu? You want see how we do for you? We play, we do fun. If you want, we can do more. If you no like girl, maybe you want boy?

—No boys.

She leans in, her tongue playing at her lips – You want to watch friend eat my pussy?

Two men walk through the doorway, small bony-framed Cambodians with sparse moustaches, plastic sandals. Booze. Greasy undershirts. One man walks directly for the wide-nose girl – a torrent of Khmer – he grabs her arm and pulls her towards the back room. Wide-nose screams, her fingernails flared into his shoulder. She yanks away from him, runs and drapes her arm around my neck.

—Tonight you stay with me! You stay. That man no good! Say you stay with me!

Undershirt-man pauses, then totters over to me with blood-shot eyes, his dark skin oily from the heat and unwash. He spits and brings his face so close I see the concrete dust clinging to the fibres of his moustache. Stink of long camel teeth. The smell of his armpit, cough, a phlegm wad chewed then spat. *He ask if you have weapon.* No weapon. Not in the saving business.

Shlomi says – That's west of the lake. I hear you aren't sup-posed to go there. No thanks, I'll stay here – he licks the Rizla closed.

—Where'd you hear that?

—That's what all the guidebooks say. You should pay more attention to what they write in there. They're trying to warn you so you don't get yourself hurt. This is my vacation and I don't want to get rolled up in a lot of shit. Here it's not like Israel, or Canada, wherever. Things can get serious. You can't walk around at night and trust people's manners will keep you safe.

—Piat is taking me.

—And what do you think he'll do for you if you end up in shit? You think he'll put his ass on the line to keep some tourist from getting killed? Nice guy, sure, but not about to lose his skin over you. Yeah? You smoked this weed before?

—You think I shouldn't go?

—Go if you want, just don't forget where you are. This stuff is great, smells strong as shit.

Twenty-two, fresh from mandatory army service, tanned with near-black Israeli scruff, a shaved head, shirtless, red jogging shorts. He lights the joint and passes it to me – You've been to Angkor?

—Brilliant, yeah, but crowded with touts. Not even a moment to just let it soak in without some kid trying to sell you postcards. Everyone scrambling on top of the temples for the sunset, rich ones on elephants, beggars lined up with all their amputations displayed. You've got to see it but the place is a circus really.

—Why you think that?

—Siem Reap is like a giant theme park. Five-star hotels, limousines...

—I mean, why must I see it?

—See Angkor?

—Yes, why must I see this thing everyone tells me I must see? Why must I take a photo of something everyone else has the same photo of?

Pause.

Pause because he's right. Because he's twenty-two. Because it all suddenly hits me that memories end up piled and forgotten like postcards anyway, because it's just another form of capture, because I've got a right to go wherever I like in this sad little country.

—Because it's Angkor - I say - And you don't come to Cambodia and not see Angkor...

—Fuck it - Shlomi says.

—What do you mean, fuck it?

—Fuck having to go to Angkor. Do I really miss out on anything besides what everyone else has already seen?

Cheap Charlie, he's right. I've been conned. Sucker.

The Killing Fields plays for the third time in the background. Shlomi looks over his shoulder and then lays his head on his arms on the table.

I say - Fuck, that joint did me in too. What's it like in Israel anyway? Ever shoot a man with your gun? - and then stub the roach out in the plastic lid of the water bottle.

A knock on my door grabs at the edges of my sleep. The clock reads six-thirty, the voices of the women murmuring through the walls, already in the kitchen for hours. I open the door and a small girl with dirty feet is standing in the doorway. Fourteen, maybe twelve.

—Hey, mister. You let me in? You want feel sex ten minutes cheap price? - her hand shoots up the leg of my boxer shorts.

—What? Jesus Christ. No.

From the empty hallway, the first light of dawn already seeps like grey dishwater. She came directly from the street or wanting a few more bucks after the last traveller upstairs or next door.

—Come on - she pleads at me softly - Only ten minutes. Why you don't want?

I close the door in her face. Like a stray dog, her biscuit dropped and sagging tail. It's not worth the potential damage. Door to door, so early and barefoot. I wonder where she came from, who she finds next, what her options are and if I've just exhausted them.

Khoi sighs and says - Now Cambodia have many problem. But before, Cambodia have *big* problem.

He walks to the edge of the wooden deck and looks out over the lake at the distant lights of the Tuol Kork district. The hyacinth continents drift and gather, a Pangaea dispersing and congealing according to tide and surface winds. Boeng Kak, the urban lake and stagnant bladder of Phnom Penh.

—The Khmer Rouge?

Khoi half smiles - Why does every tourist like so much the Khmer Rouge? Every day they want to see *Killing Fields* and Tuol Sleng prison. Sometime I think Khmer Rouge is very good for Cambodia.

Politely, sarcastically, empathetically, I laugh - And the tourists?

—They just tourists, you know. They have lots of money, they give our place good business. I work at this guesthouse so I don't mind about tourists. This is my job, you know, to pay for school, to get good money. Then I will travel to America and Portugal, one day even Uganda!

The hyacinth clumps pause in their break from the wooden posts. The water laps as Khoi says – My father die, you know. I live with my mother, my grandmother, two sister, two brother. Khmer Rouge come and look in our house, under the floor. They say we keep too much rice, they say we hide it. My father tell them no, but they keep looking for rice. They can't find it, you know, because we don't have. Then they take my father.

—Where'd they take him?

Khoi shrugs – I was a boy. Past is past. Nobody here thinks about Khmer Rouge anymore, just the future. People want good things, and good things come from China. You look at something and if it say 'Made in China' it's much better than 'Made in Cambodia.' Look at your iPod. It says 'Made in China.' Sure!

—But people died.

—Sure! That's a life, people die! But now I work to save money for school. I meet tourists and if they want to go to cock-fighting or shooting range, I take them. If they want a bus ticket to Siem Reap or Sihanoukville, I buy for them. But for some reason they always ask about Khmer Rouge. I think – My God! We have Angkor Wat in this country! Why not ask about that!

*Year Zero. Emptied streets of the capital, laundry on lines
strung between deserted apartments. Glorious restart of civilization: The city dwellers marched along the highways out
into the countryside, hospital beds poured out, newspapers
careening down the abandoned sidewalks with no traffic to
stop them like birds with propaganda wings. A forced evacua-
tion, all of Phnom Penh empty as marrowless bone.*

—A girl knocked on my door this morning.

Shlomi picks up the binoculars and peers out across the
lake at the boys in the canoe.

—Ten minutes, she said. She had her hand up my shorts
and Christ, I had to shove her out. Six-thirty in the morning.
For some reason, I thought she was being chased.

—That was a dream?

—No, very real.

—Every day, for hours and hours. What do they do when
the rain comes?

Piat's motorcycle growls beneath us and pulls out into the
alleyway leading from the guesthouse. I want to get lost in this
city with its corners of orange carts, soldier-guarded bank
machines, hundreds of parked motorcycles lined up outside the
market, patient as cattle. Bicycles, guns, cement buildings with
their corners held up by precarious scaffolds, workmen in bare
feet ferrying baskets of crushed stone. We weave between
trucks and then sit in thick exhaust at stoplights. I study the
back of Piat's brown neck, the afternoon heat blazing heavy on
my own. From the upper-story apartments, curtains blow like
ghosts out towards the farmland.

We turn off the main road into a tidy division of parallel streets, each towering with open-windowed apartments, flowerpots, the smell of fruit peels forgotten in the sun. Snug behind a row of pink flowering shrubs and neat lines of palm trees, a low three-storey school building sits on its manicured lawn: Tuol Sleng prison, S-21 concentration camp, a former high school turned torture headquarters still with its nets of barbed wire guarding the open-air hallways.

—What do you want to go there for? - Shlomi's leg dangles from the hammock - Why are people so fascinated by killing? It's the same with the Jews. Everywhere these memorials where people have been murdered. All their names and their pictures. It's like suffering in multiple lifetimes, I don't need to visit a place like that. There's nothing worth remembering about killing. It's not like the movies where the good guy shoots the bad guy. When there's war people die. It's not so clean as you think.

—Okay, so stay here. But history happened. Being reminded of our mistakes prevents them from happening again.

—Bullshit - he says - Is that what you think? With all our shrines to terrible things, you think we think twice before killing again? Israelis, we should know better! We should let these people heal and stop...whatever...picking the scab.

Wide-nose girl digs her fingernails into my arm as we walk towards the back room along a narrow, dead-end hallway with peeling black doors. Now in different light, I see the roughened texture of her skin, her clusters of acne, her eyes shadowed with dark aureoles - That guy no good! Everyday he try come and stay with me. Sometimes I do with him but now I don't want. Now you stay with me!

Filthy as a psych-ward mattress, this whole business of buying and selling. Hot fluid exchange, drip and stain, rodent viruses that chew canals into immunity linings then burst with swarms of shit-flies. And not even that, not simply the sickness, even if this whole thing was sanitized of danger, still that roar of want – teeth grinding, hold-her-down-until-I-finish, chopper blades thrusting through the sound barrier over enemy territory, small hand up the leg of my boxer shorts, *want feel sex ten minutes cheap price*. Our law. Their law. The toll it must take and all I'm responsible for.

Inside the room, wide-nose takes her shoes off. Holes litter the toes of her stockings. Gold earrings bounce against her cheeks, her skirt clasp strains beneath her belly – I happy tonight you stay with me. That guy before, no good. What you want, handsome? – she takes off her shirt revealing two Asian breasts rorschached with bruises – Come here, I give you head.

—It's okay...don't worry about it.

—You no like? You want I call my friend?

—No. Don't do that.

—You watch me fuck myself?

—Jesus Christ, I don't want anything.

—What?

—I said don't worry about it. Let's just sit and wait here.

The makeup on her face flexes in offence – So stupid. Piece-of-shit Cheap Charlie! Why you come here, you no want something?

—I just want to sit. That's what I want.

—I think maybe you want boy.

Concrete wall, metal bed frame, her brown body under the fluorescent bulb. This room is a strange underworld cavern I've surfaced in. Not my territory. Shining armour bullshit. Definitely not in the saving business. From behind the walls, the rhythmic creak of a rusted bed shifting positions, smell of wet skunk weed, water hyacinth, diesel fumes. The girl picks at her toenails through the holes in her stockings. After ten minutes, the sound of Cambodian rap translated through plywood.

I come out into the red-lit room again. Piat waits at the bar with the two girls. The lesbians and Cambodian men have disappeared.

—You like my honeys? On my life! Tonight I cum so quick!

—Take me back to the guesthouse.

—How was the prison? – Shlomi says from behind his sunglasses, his shoulders tanned, reclined on a chair pulled out on the wooden deck soaking up the afternoon breeze off the lake.

—How you'd expect. Barbed wire still, bloodstains on the floor. Nothing moved or changed. A horrible feeling of ghosts...thousands and thousands.

A girl from the kitchen brings him a plate of fried rice and a coconut milkshake.

—I don't know why you wanted to go there – he scoffs – It's like taking your vacation at Auschwitz.

Khoi calls from the bar – Hey! Some guy gave me his iPod. You show me how it works? My iPod is your iPod. My wife, your wife!

The sun disappears behind the storm clouds. Rain patters on the wooden deck. We move the table and chair inside beneath a growl of thunder. Out on the lake the boys paddle to shore as the storm pulls closer. Suspended on heavy clouds, lightning shudders loose from their insides. On the street everyone on motorbikes is draped in plastic raincoats, tails of muddy street water spraying up behind them. Monsoon season. Tropical laundry day.

—Bought some weed from Piat this morning. He's surprised me, that guy. Just a kid but sure knows how to make a sale.

The sky is dark now. The air smells fresh and cooler. The rain bullets down onto the tin roof, hard enough to wash stains from prison floors, to release bones caught in the ground still hung with the rags of their clothes.

—I'll roll it.

—Do you want to come to the girlie bar tonight? It's somewhere over in Tuol Kork district. More entertaining than the prison, I hope. I've never been to a bar like that before, but it's supposed to have some shows you don't forget. Ping-pong balls, birds, razor blades.

Khoi – Hey! Come see my iPod!

—That's west of the lake. You aren't supposed to go there – Shlomi says, licking the Rizla closed – No thanks, I'll stay here.

Finally I say good-night to Khoi, passing the chalkboard beside the darkened bar: *Tonight – Killing Fields 7 pm.* Going to my three-dollar room hung with a pink mosquito net sticky with smoke resin, my bathroom still wet from the shower this morning, a smell I recognize from back in the Mekong Delta: swampland, cracked plastic soap dish, toilet roll soggy with condensation, I feel the entire weight of the city's history press down on me. Ghosts like grease marks on painted plywood. Lying in bed beneath the growl of street traffic, there's always that dread of making things worse, having left a more permanent stain. Year Zero. Jesus Christ. *What do you want to go there for?* This isn't my territory, done wandering through smoldering villages, climbing Angkor with all the tourist hoards, smug and empathetic. Wide-nose women never heard of being saved. What if I had let her in this morning? Just given her a few hundred riel, made sure she wasn't being chased. Tiny hand up the leg of my boxer shorts, piece-of-shit Cheap Charlie, *my God*, how does this all happen? The cost of one bullet, that blood on the prison floor, flared nostrils, Khoi riding the water buffalo through the emerald rice fields as the soldiers search his house and the rain clouds drift over.

Les 3 Chevaliers remains etched on a wall in S-21 prison. It means "the three knights."

THE STAMPEDE

The police had already cordoned off the entrance to the rocky path that snaked four kilometres up to the Naina Devi temple. A crowd had gathered along the road and most of them were crying, throwing their arms up in the air and forcing the stiff-backed policemen to restrain them from running up the trail. Carter looked out over the valley and then to the flashing lights of the ambulances and wondered if being crushed under a stampede felt anything like knowing about what he knew but not being able to stop it.

—*Maybe she won't do it* - he thought - *She's only trying to scare me. That's how it works.*

It was unlikely, but he thought it anyway.

From the base of the hill, Carter could see out over the roofs of the houses that were stacked up the side of the valley to the road where the cars were parked. Farther in the distance low peaks emerged, patched with orchards and meadow-like carpets of wild flowers. They weren't marigolds; their petals were the same colour but with stems that seemed as though they would break more easily. The base of the hills was stepped in terraces of rice and as the emerald slopes rose, their colour faded to brown from the scree and then to white where the snowy tips of the Himachal Pradesh disappeared into wisps of cloud.

Om Prakash stood next to Carter – I believe I have the beginning, sir. Please tell me if you like it – then he read from a notepad that shook slightly in his hand – *One hundred forty-five Hindu pilgrims were trampled to death during a stampede at a northern Indian temple...*

—No, no – Carter interrupted – You can't begin like that. *Trampled* makes them sound like cattle.

—Cattle, sir?

—Were they trampled by cattle?

—No, sir. By other people.

—Prakash, the world won't tolerate Indians being written about like that anymore. Maybe in the fifties you could get away with it, but not now. No more *memsahib* or tiger hunts, you know that, right? The sun never sets and all that? Begin with how their clothes are brightly coloured.

—Brightly coloured...

—That way it's not all chaos, you see. Now it's all engineers and hydro dams, female doctors and such. At least that's what they want you to believe, Prakash. Seems everyone's forgotten that most of India is still a poor garbage heap.

Carter felt the muscles in his stomach clench and the air rush from his lungs as he remembered again and wondered whether or not she would go through with it. The feeling was involuntary. Like a sudden nausea that wakes you in the dead of sleep, he was at the feeling's mercy. She had promised she would do it and even though she had said it all from spite, the look in her eyes had said – *I'd do it just to prove I would.*

—No panic then?

—What?

—A stampede is about panic, sir.

—Right. Of course there should be panic...

—My wish is to preserve the accuracy of the event. I would not like to lose sight of what really happened.

Om Prakash spoke deliberately and respectfully. Carter appreciated that but didn't like how long this was taking. Reuters had a strict deadline for filing evening reports and he wanted this article taken care of before they returned to Delhi. Carter took a drink from his water bottle, closed his eyes, and wondered if he could still make it back in time to catch the overnight flight to London.

—*Maybe there's time* – he thought – *If we hurry, there might just be time.*

He spoke to Om Prakash, who had started writing in his notepad again.

—Do you have a wife, Prakash?

—A wife?

—Or are you engaged to be with someone?

Prakash blushed – No, sir. I do not have a wife.

Carter looked out at the peaks of the mountains – A male friend then? A buddy or something?

Prakash's blush deepened – No, sir. That is not even legal in India, if that is what you mean.

—It should be – Carter said – Things might be a lot easier for you.

He looked at Prakash and wondered if he might be lying.

—That man in the blue shirt and white dhoti, do you see him?

—Yes.

—That one over there.

—Yes, sir.

The man stood wailing in the shade of a tree, his hands pressed to his face. He had a moustache and was shaking his head distraughtly at something being said to him.

—That man claims there were rumours of landslides...

—Landslides?

—Because of the rain. Write that – Carter said – *Incessant rains had loosened the soil and rumours of landslides startled the crowd...*

—With all due respect, sir, *startled* sounds like cattle too.

—Does it? Maybe if I had said *spooked* I could see that, but *startled* seems appropriate. Hard work getting this right, isn't it, Prakash? Are you sure you want to be a journalist?

Om Prakash looked at him – Yes, sir.

—There will always be difficult things in life. A journalist must try to portray them all correctly to the world. Passionately, but correctly. That's the job. You think you can do that?

—Yes, sir. I'd like to interview a family member, if you wouldn't mind.

—Fine, Prakash, but make sure they're upset. You'll need a strong headline.

Om Prakash walked over to the group of mourners and began speaking with an old woman. Carter watched her as she wailed and thought – *What should I believe? That she was only threatening to leave me? That she said so as a last resort? Goddammit. Prakash should hurry up. I could get back to Delhi and be in London by tomorrow.*

Carter knew he deserved it if she left, but the pain in his stomach didn't seem fair. All this churning inside him didn't seem fair at all. He looked out over the valley, and in the distance he could barely make out a tiny hut sitting on the edge of a green rice field. A thread of grey smoke spiraled into the air from some sort of rubbish fire and for a moment he deeply envied whoever lived there – *Why does everything have to be so complicated?*

Carter watched Om Prakash write furiously in his note-book as the crowd of mourners gathered around him, each eager to cry out their version of the events. Prakash took tiny steps back on the gravel and every time the crowd inched forward. He could understand the disgust of the British but he wasn't allowed to say it. His job was to report the news and to keep personal opinions to himself. India was becoming too difficult to write about these days. One had to be so careful.

The police carried the dead bodies down from the temple and were lining them up at the guardrail near the edge of the cliff. Carter looked at his watch – *Dammit, Prakash. Hurry up.*

Om Prakash turned his back to the mourners and wiped his forehead with the sleeve of his shirt. He walked over to Carter and said – They say the guardrail broke. Many people fell to their deaths, it seems.

—So they weren't trampled after all?

—Some were. Others fell, sir. One woman said she saw her children... - Prakash read from his notebook - ...*tumbling down the hillside.*

—Terrible - Carter said - But make sure you mention those children.

—One man lost all three. He said to me, 'I fail to see why God was so cruel.'

Cruelty is relative - Carter thought - *There are many ways for the gods to be cruel.* He looked at Om Prakash and said - You see there, a fine headline.

—Such a tragedy - Om Prakash said, looking out at the valley - to be trampled under human feet. There are too many horrible things in the world. Aren't there, sir? Does a journalist ever grow tired of seeing them all?

Carter looked at the tiny hut in the distance. The sun had begun to tilt the shadow of the mountains towards where Carter and Prakash were standing, but a gap of silver light remained between them. Carter mentally marked the sun's boundary with a boulder resting at its edge. He forced himself to reply.

—A journalist must never become tired of the truth, Prakash. Our job is to show others what they're unable to see for themselves. Isn't that right?

Carter looked back at the boulder hoping the sun had moved. It had, but only slightly. He looked at Om Prakash again - I'm going to ask you a personal question.

—Yes, sir.

Carter hesitated and then said – Where will you go tonight, once we're back in Delhi?

—You mean for dinner, sir?

—Well, yes. That. But more generally too. What I mean is, will you sleep alone?

—Sir?

—Alone...as in by yourself. Never mind, Prakash. You're an idiot sometimes. I really think so.

She was going to break his heart; he should resign himself to that. He should prepare himself so that when he returned to London and she wasn't there, he would be ready.

—*I should never have let myself care about anyone in the first place* – he thought. His stomach still felt coiled in knots and he could feel it all thudding in his chest.

—If you must know, sir – Om Prakash said – I will sleep alone tonight. And tomorrow night and the night after that. For myself, sir, I think this is the safest way for a man to live.

—Perhaps – Carter said – You could damn well be right about that.

—Yes, sir.

—And you didn't have girlfriends in school?

—No, sir. I studied and played cricket mostly.

—Better that way. Women love a cricketer, don't they? – he turned towards the sound of the wailing again.

—I don't know, sir.

—But a shame to sleep alone...

—Sir?

Carter didn't answer.

By the time Om Prakash had finished, the mountain's shadow stretched well beyond the boulder. The police began to load the bodies into ambulances that were driven down the hill to the hospital in Shimla. Carter watched Om Prakash as he walked over to the driver of the car they had hired in Delhi. He would have to pay him extra for staying longer. They would be too late now to make it back in time for a flight to London. She would have left and he would be too late to stop her. Carter's face felt oily and his shirt stuck to his back where the sweat had pooled. Prakash's brown skin looked dry and clean by contrast.

—*She would have done it by now* – he thought. He would go back to London and she would have done it like she'd threatened to. Carter watched Prakash gather their things and pack them into the car.

—*Not a bad-looking man* – Carter thought – *But not nearly bright enough to ever make it as a journalist.*

They would be back in Delhi in a few hours and Prakash would leave to eat dinner alone. Carter would file the story to Reuters, take a cool shower and then lay on his bed in his towel. Slowly, at the bottom of his stomach, the panic would begin to expand: If she was gone, he would be alone.

And then what?

A Severed Arm

Bosh looked over his shoulder, back into the rustling damp of the jungle. The trees and bushes were alive with a nighttime chorus of insects that made it all sound like busted machinery.

—That's the wrong sound – he said – You listen, Miles. Tell me if that isn't the wrong sound.

Miles pretended not to hear him and continued shaving the husk of an empty coconut with the rusted machete.

Bosh said – Hey! – and chucked a handful of sand at Miles' lap – I said the jungle's making the wrong sound. What're you deaf or something?

—Leave it – I said – There isn't anything we can do now. The jungle makes all sorts of noises when you just leave it be.

Bosh stared at Miles shaving the coconut – Christ, doesn't he look like he'll kill you?

Miles said – I won't kill anyone.

—Ha! – Bosh said – Won't kill anyone. Would you listen to that noise? Jungle's out to eat somebody tonight. That's the wrong sound, Carl, isn't it?

I said it sounded different from other nights, but nothing so bad it could have torn us apart in our sleep or changed what we were planning on doing that night. At least not before the boat came. Probably not before the boat came.

Anchored offshore between our island and that of Ko Yao shone the lights of the army boat, a full-sized troop carrier squatting in the water of the channel. It sat there, fat and omnipotent, its radar spinning silently on top like it knew something we didn't. On its deck, dim outlines of soldiers paused by the railings with mouths full of cigarettes and quick Thai. They congregated in groups, coughed and adjusted their hats, staring out onto the beach of Ko Yao and probably up the whole Malay Peninsula all the way to Bangkok.

—Must be flooded by now – Bosh stared at the island, bobbing his head to the dull thud of the techno beat that carried over – I hope you got the stuff hidden well, Carl. They've brought in the army. They mean business.

I said – It's fine. We won't get searched. There are ten thousand people on that beach, no one's going to bother us.

Bosh said – You can tell those army boys are aching for a catch of drugged-up *farang*. Remember how they strip-search in Thailand, Miles? Want me to show you?

Miles said – Fuck off.

—They don't change gloves, see. They bend you over, grease your crack with jelly and stick it in you, same glove as the guy before.

Miles kept shaving the coconut.

—Looking for drugs and weapons mostly. You never heard of that? That's how they do it here.

Bosh nodded his head with the techno beat again. It drifted over the water like the muffled cough of a clock. Miles dug the tip of the machete into the sand and stood up. Hairs from the coconut stuck to his shorts.

—I'm going to check for the boat – he said, and walked off towards the boulders.

—If you don't come back, what'll we tell your folks? – Bosh hollered at Miles' back – Should we tell 'em you fucked a twelve-year-old then gave her the wrong currency as payment? – He began to laugh – Remember, Carl? Should we tell 'em that, Miles? Huh? Want us to pass that on to the family? Christ, what a shit-dick.

Miles disappeared over the line of boulders that cut down the beach from the jungle into the water. Bosh laughed as he picked up the machete.

—Remember that, Carl? Tried to give her riel instead of baht and she just stood there and the kid wouldn't take it! And the kid's mother was watching all the time from the corner trying to teach her how to take what she'd earned, but she was too shy after the whole thing so she just stood there not taking it. And Miles looking like he just wanted to get the hell out of there, but the kid won't take the money!

—I know the story – I said.

—So he sets the bills down at her feet and goes to leave, but her mother comes walking over...

—I know the story.

—...and picks up the bills and says, what did she say, Carl, come on.

—Fuck off.

—What'd she say! Come on, she picks up the bills and says what?

—You're a miserable cunt, you know that, Bosh?

—What'd she say!

—You're a cunt, Bosh. A real cunt.

—She picks up the bills and says... - Bosh bent over double, trying to speak between his laughter - 'Dis Thailand, assho'! - then he exploded like a dropped drawer of cutlery. Maniacally he hacked at the sand with the machete and the jungle buzz rose through the thick screen of air until every vibration landed on our skin like caterpillars dancing back to their cocoons.

Across the water, the shore of Ko Yao blazed like a fiery horizon that sent electric ripples out as far as the hull of the army boat. A dozen soldiers on deck leaned over the railings and were spitting into the black water. I couldn't see for sure but that's our tendency, to wait and watch and appreciate the impact. I pictured the inside of the ship, the cramped bunk rooms with legs dangling from tiered beds, the air thick with feet and cigarettes, the low gurgles of Thai echoing off the hull down into the dark water.

—Gonna be one hell of a party - Bosh said - Why they got the boat sitting there? Wonder what's going on.

I said - I heard some kid got stabbed a few nights ago. Army's there just to make sure.

—Bastards - Bosh said - I hope you got it hidden well, Carl. I wasn't kidding about the strip search. They'd fuck us over long-time if we showed up in prison here. Twenty years for a single pill. You get caught with more they'll lop you into pieces and eat you with chopsticks. I can understand why they think we're always looking for trouble, Carl. But we're not here to hurt anyone or steal anything. Just want to swim a little, smoke a few joints in a hammock, dance on the beach with the full moon. That's what we pay for and we pay for what we take. A fair agreement, don't you think? Then they come bringing in a goddamn army boat.

I saw Miles drop down from the boulders, his feet sending up sprays of sand behind him as he walked towards us.

—Met four others over there, all waiting for a boat – he said – Two Germans, a British girl and a Roman with a missing arm.

—A Roman? – Bosh said – Yeah right.

—Said he's from Rome.

—They're called Italians – I said – The Romans were of the Empire, nobody wants to remember that.

—He's missing an arm.

—An arm? – Bosh said. He hacked at the sand with the machete. I could see him aim for the scuttling shell of a hermit crab that ran sideways between the falling blade on its way back to its tunnel.

Bosh said – I wonder where he left it... – and suddenly brought an end to his chopping – How do you lose your goddamn arm? – He examined the skewered hermit crab.

—I don't think... - Miles started, but Bosh had already stood up and was walking towards the water, dangling the machete from its handle like he didn't want to touch it. He walked in up to his knees, then bent down and rinsed the blade in the ripples of light from the army boat. I wondered if he ever remembered anything he said. He looked like an old Thai fisherman skimming for crayfish in the soggy twilight, doomed to come back to his fire and eat them alone.

—Did you tell him? – Miles said.

—I didn't say anything. It isn't my problem.

—You're feeling okay about this, aren't you? You want me to take it? I've carried stuff before, I know how it goes.

—No – I said – I lost the bet, I'll take them.

—Don't mind about that.

—I lost the bet, so I'll carry them.

Bosh walked back and dropped the machete beside me. It was wet and the sand exploded over it like a virus. He stood with his back to the jungle, as though trying to avoid giving it eye contact, but you could see in his face he was listening to the noises and thinking they were all wrong.

Bosh said – I'm going to see where that boat is. I've got a feeling it's not coming tonight. Probably forgotten all about us. Have to sit and just stare at the goddamn island, that goddamn fucking army boat...

He took a few steps towards the boulders then stopped and turned to face the water, nodded his head with the techno beat then turned again and disappeared over the rocks.

When Bosh had gone, I stared out at the shore of Ko Yao and then at the army boat. A small, low vessel the size of a fishing boat pulled up alongside the metal hull and soldiers climbed a rope ladder down into it. When it was full, the boat pulled away and motored towards the electrified strip of beach.

I said – What do you really think they're up to?

Miles said – Patrolling for drug boats. Fishermen drive them up along the coast bringing cargo in from Cambodia for the parties. Doesn't seem to do any good though. More ecstasy floats around that beach than the epicentre of a mosque – Then he paused and said quietly with something sharp rasping at his vocal chords – Carl, I never would have done it. I just wasn't thinking, you know? Too much stuff going on all at once and I wasn't thinking. I didn't know she was twelve and now I've got that to hold onto for the rest of my life, and then all that shit about paying her right...

I said – It's not so bad – because I felt it was the nicest thing to say. Then I felt the baggie rolled up in my pocket and saw the milky forehead of the moon lift above the top of Ko Yao, its reflection mixing its tentacles with the lights from the beach and the army boat and I wondered what it would be like to be him with all that shit to carry.

—It is bad – Miles said – I have to drag that memory around now and Bosh always reminding me. He won't let it go and that makes it impossible.

I said – You won't always remember. She won't either – But I figured Miles could tell I was lying.

—And Bosh?

—Bosh will forget soon enough.

—The truth is – Miles said – I didn't even want to. It was Bosh's idea, the whole thing. He said it was too dangerous in

Phnom Penh because they weren't used to us there and the girls wouldn't know how to take precautions. But when we came here they just pulled us off the street and started jabbering on about how cheap it was and I thought I'd just get it over with since Bosh wouldn't let up about doing it at least once before we left.

—Once you're home – I lied – you won't remember. You leave all that stuff here – but I was thinking to myself that's one thing you don't want to get stuck with. Then I remembered how it was hard to tell what people carried around and it didn't all make sense if you just looked at them one way. Then I wondered what people thought I was stuck with and if it made any difference. And then I wondered about Bosh too.

Miles and I sat facing the water and watched the moon open itself fully into the sky above Ko Yao. There were three or four techno beats now, thumping against each other discordantly, synchronizing for a moment before pulling apart like someone clapping just out of rhythm at a campfire. Each of us has our shit, I thought.

Bosh appeared on the boulders and stood there for a moment before jumping down into the sand.

He walked over and sat down, picked up the machete and said – Lost it to gangrene.

—Lost what? – I said.

—His arm. The Roman, he lost it to gangrene. I went and talked to the guys waiting for the boat and I asked him, 'Where did you lose your arm?' and he said, 'In Borneo.' He was in the jungle on some tourist trek and he got separated from his group. He tripped and fell over a cliff and broke his arm. Big gash, open wound, everything. He goes wandering around the jungle for eight days until he gets to this village where a medicine man tries to treat him. Puts some herbal shit on the wound, sets it with bamboo, feeds him by hand since he has a fever, until someone from the nearest town can come and get him. By that time he's delirious and his arm is beginning to fester. Says mosquito larvae had burrowed into him. Says it was already beginning to rot by the time they flew him to Jakarta. Says he passed out when the doctor examined it and by the time he woke, it was gone. Lost it to gangrene.

Bosh sat proudly, like he wanted to say *that's that*, like he had deciphered a wall of hieroglyphs and we didn't know enough to prove to him otherwise. I thought about the Roman and wondered what he thought when he looked down and saw the wound for the first time. I pictured the black moss of gangrene creeping from the stump of amputation and what they do with an arm once it's been severed. What happens here is different, I thought, and I thought of telling Miles to make him feel better but didn't.

The noise of the jungle grew louder and I finally agreed with Bosh that it sounded wrong, that away from the guesthouse restaurant with the pool table, with the illuminated threads of smoke spooling upward by the lazy draw of the ceiling fan, with the wet bottles of beer in tanned hands that rested on tanned bellies, I could hear the jaws of the insects gnash their discontent at us from their hidden bark perches. I wondered if the Roman had heard the same thing when he looked down and saw it.

Then over the boulders a figure dropped into the sand and before we could see who it was, it called to us – The boat is coming – and I looked at the silhouette to see if there was an arm missing but it was too far away to tell. Bosh and Miles stood and brushed off their shorts and I stood and took the machete by the handle and hung it from my belt.

The driver of the boat steered using his calloused foot to move the tiller, and he aimed with his eyes towards the bright strip of beach all of us watched grow closer like the lights of an unknown city our plane slowly descended into. Two Germans sat at the bow and tried lighting cigarettes against the wind. The British girl sat between Bosh and Miles and said – The island was lovely, wasn't it? – when I helped her into the boat. I sat next to the Roman on purpose to see what he did without an arm and if he still noticed it wasn't there.

He said his name was Marco and I said – Gangrene, eh? – and he said yes like he was used to the question. The stub showed slightly from beneath his T-shirt so I sat on that side of him to show it didn't bother me.

One of the Germans shouted to us – Ever been to this party? – and Bosh shouted back that we hadn't, and the Germans smiled and asked if we had ever heard of anyone getting caught.

—No – Bosh said – But some kid got stabbed a few nights ago. That's how come the army boat.

The full moon hovered above the broken ridge of Ko Yao and as we passed by the large metal hull, a boat of troops pushed off and drove beside us towards the island. I could see their Thai faces and the green of their uniforms, and I saw the difference between our two boats that sped over the reflections of the moon and the island like two competing striders on a puddle of oil. Above the roar of the motor I could hear the techno beats thumping from speakers tied high around the necks of the palm trees on shore, and as we drove closer I could see the stiff uniforms of the soldiers moving deliberately through the crowds and I started to feel nervous. Bosh and the two Germans nodded their heads with the beat and Bosh looked back over his shoulder and gave me a grin that said *This is gonna be real!* The British girl was smiling sweetly and I suddenly felt old and sick and heavy. Miles was staring at the bottom of the boat and not even at Ko Yao at all. You knew, I thought. That's why you can't forget. You knew from the beginning and now you're stuck with it.

I reached into my pocket and gripped the baggie in my hand and I looked over at the water still full of throbbing reflections.

What if I told them I lost it, I thought. I could always say I lost it.

By now you could see the full scope of the party. Tens of thousands of people danced on the sand to the music from the speakers. Some crawled into the waves with their clothes on, or staggered at the break of the surf to puke or pull their shorts down to piss. There were layers of people coating each bar that lined the beach, smothering the steps and the railings, up the balconies onto the roof so the whole thing looked alive as with giant termites. There were fire spinners with their eyes closed, groups of men fumbling with the clasp of a woman's bra, some-one standing in the water bleeding from a neck wound, his friends shouting in English to a guy shouting back in Thai. Whole boats packed with travellers were arriving from other beaches. They pulled up and disappeared into the party the way spit suddenly sinks into sand. Between the dancers, the steady green of the army uniforms were patrolling the whole thing and I felt sick as I held the bag in my pocket.

Bosh looked over his shoulder again and grinned as the boat slid up onto the beach. *This is gonna be real!*

I thought, what if I just say I lost it...

CRAWLING WITH THIEVES

There were temples at both ends of the main dirt road in town. One was an enormous stone complex with eight massive towers, standing strong and immovable. People in colourful saris and men with combed moustaches streamed in carrying bags of marigolds and coconuts. They exited with their dark foreheads dotted red or yellow or streaked with white, and continued along the cracked sidewalk in their bare feet. At the opposite end, a kilometre or so towards the hills, the road disappeared into grass on its way to a massive stone pavilion that housed a sixteen-foot statue of Nandi the bull. Behind the pavilion, stone steps wound up the dry hill and then disappeared behind clusters of sandy boulders. Above it all, the clouds sat quietly in the blue sky as if proof some lid had been arched and sealed over the whole thing. The tall weeds stood still against the columns of the ruins and the soft hooves of the cows thumped gently as they inched their noses forward to new grass.

I walked from the centre of town towards the statue of the bull wondering if Cassie had stopped crying yet and if she had figured out a way to make sense of everything despite it not getting any better. All last night she had been on the brink of tears, saying it was too much for her and for Christ's sake none of it was fair.

I said – No. Nothing's fair – but we couldn't do anything about it this day or the next or anytime soon if we expected to fix the whole goddamned thing.

—Goddamned is right – she blew her nose – Goddamned is right.

This morning she stayed in bed as I went to find breakfast. She lay beneath the mosquito netting looking like some malarial sub-Saharan, though it was her mind not her body that had given up.

—I could hear everything you did in the bathroom – she lay curled on the bed.

I said – It can't be helped. I feel better now though. I'm going to eat breakfast and then walk to the river. Sure you don't want to come?

—I can't face it again – she said – Actually, I want to leave.

—We're not leaving. You should get out of bed at least. Look around the shops or something.

—No – she said – I don't want to see any more of it.

Out towards the statue, children played cricket on the dry ground where the road disappeared into grass. Farther on, the cows stood and watched dumbly. The children batted and then ran in bare feet. I wanted to take my shoes off and run with them but their soles were worn thick as elephants' and could tolerate the scalding earth. Beneath the stone pavilion, the weathered face of Nandi stared down the street to the towers of the far temple. Along the edges of the road, chickens darted from the shade; colourful racks of clothing and jewelry shimmered behind the heat, and there was no other movement except when a child would swing the cricket bat.

Where the grass disappeared, the road forked left through the forest down towards the river. It was cooler in the shade. At the junction there were a few people sitting by the trees on old logs behind their ramshackle carts selling water or juice or biscuits. No one looked up as I passed except a young boy who stood next to his cart. I was glad to be out of Bangalore and into the countryside. There had been too many dishonest people and the men on the street had laughed and taunted Cassie when she'd worn her sari incorrectly. Bangalore was an old city that seemed to have been recently suctioned. Everything loose had disappeared.

On the forest road ahead of me, three young men slowed and turned to watch me coming. They whispered to each other as I got closer and I wondered what it was about.

I thought – What's the worst that could happen? Robbery? Knives? Poison? – and kept walking without slowing down. As I passed them, one stuck out his hand to shake mine and told me I was from America.

I said – Not from America – and the other two men shook my hand.

Together we walked along the road beneath the trees and then down to the river.

The tallest one said – You come here alone?

I said – My wife is back at the hotel. She doesn't feel like moving.

—A tired wife. So young to be married – he said.

I said – Yes – and then – but Indians marry even younger.

The three men smiled. The tall one said – We are not married. We're students at the college of engineering.

And I thought – Ah, India rising.

As we came through the trees, the path opened out to a broad stone riverbank. Dozens of Indian families spread out along the flat rocks, their babies standing fat and naked, mothers adjusting saris that had shifted too far, the men looking stern and capable in dress pants and buttoned shirts. They were sitting in groups eating biscuits and drinking from thermoses. At the shore, several young men stood waist deep in the murky water with their longyis tied. They dipped their bodies up to the shoulders, stood, and then washed their faces vigorously with both hands. Around them, others splashed or dove out into the current and then swam back with quick strokes. Nearby, young women sat shyly with their parents and pretended not to look. Groups of Indians chatted noisily and I couldn't help but feel I had interrupted. It was so hot standing on the rocks and the river looked cool.

The three men waved for me to follow as they walked to a small gathering by the shore. They sat and pulled my arms down to sit with them and as I did, I took out some cigarettes and passed them around.

The tall one pointed to a smiling man and said – This is my brother.

The man took a cigarette, still smiling, and I smiled back.

Then he pointed to a man sitting off by himself. He had a scarf tied around his neck and his face was brown and bumpy.

—He's a thief – the tall one said, smiling.

The man looked up at me as though it were true, like he wasn't ashamed of it and was simply out of work, thanks to all the new police guarding the ruins. He picked up a stick and scratched it on the rock he was sitting on.

I thought – So that's a thief.

Cassie had said on the train from Bangalore –You know, that place is crawling with thieves. They lure you behind the boulders and throw chili in your eyes. They'll rape you twice if you scream for help. Even people in groups aren't safe. They always roam in packs.

I said – It will be fine.

And she said – It's just not fair. None of this is fair.

I said – We'll leave everything valuable in the hotel. That way they can't take anything.

—What if that's their plan? – she trembled – What if they know we leave our things behind and when we come back, it'll all be gone?

—Nothing like that will happen. Please stop saying things aren't fair.

—Well, they're not.

—There's nothing we can do about it – I said – We're here.

After an hour or two, I said goodbye to the Indians and shook their hands since they had shared their food with me. I told them of my plans to study medicine, and they were pleased to see I had a wife and had all nodded when I said we wanted children. The thief had walked away long ago and there were more questions about what it was like to study in the West and if I drove a car and how many children did I want. The afternoon sun had tilted down above the hills, and across the muddy river it was shining orange against the boulders and everything seemed safe and familiar.

I shook their hands again and walked back down the road, giving a few coins to a sadhu sitting cross-legged beneath a rock outcropping. He didn't nod or acknowledge and I kept walking. At the junction to the main dirt road, the boy beside the cart had disappeared and there were families stopped to buy water or juice or biscuits. They had come for the day from Hospet, clean and nicely dressed, and were now driving home before the sun set. The children were still playing cricket on the sparse grass; the cows had moved farther up the hill or were lying with their bodies off to one side like dogs. Nandi hadn't moved for twelve hundred years and the sun was going down for the millionth time in its presence.

When I reached the hotel, I imagined walking into the room to find Cassie gone. I thought – I hope she went out to get some food or bought a necklace at least.

Inside, Cassie was curled on the sheet beneath the mosquito net reading a book.

She said – Did you have fun? Where did you go?

I said – Down to the river. I met some Indians and sat with them. There was a thief too.

—Oh? – she put her book down.

—Did you go out?

—I didn't move. I want to leave.

—We're not leaving.

—Did you talk to the thief?

—He sat by himself. There was nothing to be afraid of.

—I'm not afraid.

—Will you at least try this? – I pulled a small bag from my pocket.

Her eyes shifted from her book to the bag then brightened and I felt happy when I saw that.

This morning at breakfast, I had asked the woman at the restaurant if she knew where I could buy some hash.

—You want hash brown? – she said.

—No – I said – Hash – I mimed smoking.

—Ashtray?

—Hash...*hash*...you know, dope?

—Ganja? – she said.

—Like ganja.

Her face was fat and young. The brown skin around her waist doubled over the band of her sari. She turned and walked to the balcony without saying anything, then yelled something to someone below.

She walked back to my table – I call my mother. You follow her.

An old woman in a green sari came up to the restaurant. Her grey hair flew out from an old braid that stretched down her back.

—Follow my mother – the woman said.

Cassie said – Where did you get it?

—This morning. I followed an old woman to someone's house. The guy spoke English. Said he could have sold me anything I wanted. Will you at least try some of it?

—Yes – Cassie said – I don't mind that. It must be dangerous to buy that here. I've heard stories of arrests for even small amounts. This is a holy town because of the ruins. They don't tolerate it here.

—It'll be fine – I said –There's nothing bad could happen.

I crawled under the mosquito net and pulled a small pipe from my pocket. When Cassie stared at it, I noticed she'd been crying. She lit the pipe and I could see her body inhale and then relax. Outside, the sun had painted the sky completely orange with edges of purple that glowed behind the roofs of the buildings beside us. We smoked until it was dark, lounging beneath the net in the warm, dusty air, and Cassie told me how she had never seen a thief before.

I said – I hadn't either. Until today.

—It must have been exciting. People who are thieves never admit it, which means he was rare.

—He didn't admit it – I said – His friends did.

—How close were you to him?

—A couple of feet.

—I wish I had gone with you. I didn't enjoy myself very much.

—Maybe tomorrow.

—Yes, I'll go out with you tomorrow. I want to climb up into those ruins. They look so pretty from down here. If we packed enough water...

—We can go to the ruins.

A few minutes later, the electricity switched off and the room became as dark as the outside. On the street a dog was barking and both Cassie and I stayed silent. I could see the red embers glowing in the bowl of the pipe. We both smoked and watched them smolder.

Then Cassie said – I have to use the toilet.

She lifted the netting and crawled down from the bed and shut the thin wooden door to the bathroom. The lights were still out but my eyes were getting used to it and I could see from the window the light of the moon on the rooftops.

Down the street a man started to yell. A door slammed and a woman began to yell. The dog barked again and the man and the woman yelled and then the woman screamed. The rest of the town was quiet. I don't know why, perhaps because the noise came from the direction of the restaurant, but I couldn't help but picture something awful happening.

—*No one was in the restaurant* – I thought – *No one else could have known* – The hash smoke had thickened the air and my face felt hot and coated. I ducked out from under the netting and lay flat out on the bare mattress. The air outside the net felt cool.

Down the street, the dog barked again and my heartbeat raced as the shouting voices travelled closer. The woman was shouting the most, and the man would be silent for a while and then shout something back.

I thought – What's the worst that could happen? The police? Arrest? Execution?

Cassie was taking so long in the bathroom, but I couldn't hear anything from behind the thin door.

Then it became clear there were two men and they both were speaking quietly but rapidly while the woman interjected with loud protests. The voices sounded no farther than ten feet away from the window. My heart started pounding and I could hear Cassie scooping water in the bathroom behind the door. The two men started to whisper but I could no longer hear the woman or the dog. Cassie came out of the bathroom and adjusted her shirt. The men suddenly stopped whispering, and in the distance I could hear the rush of the river behind the trees.

—Don't you think we should go out tonight? - she said - Let's take a walk around the town and see what's going on. There's no point in staying in, the lights won't be on for a while. Don't you think it would be exciting to walk around the town in the dark?

—No - I said - I want to stay in tonight.

—You should come out - she said.

—Cassie! - I whispered - This place is crawling with thieves!

She looked at me blankly - Don't be ridiculous. You said you had met one today and everything was fine. What's the worst that could happen?

The river rumbled in the distance, a constant rush of water dragged along the banks and reeds, smoothing the rocks and filling the water with silt.

—I'm not going anywhere tonight - I said - There's no reason to go anywhere tonight.

A FEAST OF BEAR

Polar wind ripped through the near-empty cabin as the boy lifted the hatch of the King Air turbo prop. Twenty-three thousand feet below, the bright expanse of arctic snow spread out in all directions. The two attendants, forced into retreat by the bitter cold, had tried their best to restrain him but the boy had resisted, standing at the opening as contemplative as a hiker before a canyon, peering down through the rush of cloud. Perhaps he was taking in the view of the unbounded, ice-covered tundra. Perhaps he was reconsidering the drop. But in a moment, he was gone.

—Not a chance – Jan sat up against the headboard – You can't open the door of a plane mid-flight.

—Our planes have safety features – said Connor – You'd need one hell of a grip to force it open, but you could do it. Not casually, but this guy was determined.

—One hell of a grip – Jan made a fist and flexed his forearm – You landed the plane though. Give yourself credit.

—Terry landed it. The co-pilot helps.

Jan studied Connor's grey-stubbled face. It had always interested him to watch another man in the moments following a disaster, when the thing was still raw and fibrous inside and you could watch the scene replay across the wets of his eyes. It was only then, once you'd seen that part of him, Jan felt you could know if a person was for real.

—Not many would have thought so quickly – Jan said – But you did. Always the champ.

—The cabin depressurized. It was hard to breathe.

—You still landed it.

From what Connor could remember, the boy at the door was barely twenty. Almost a man but with the smooth features of someone freshly hatched into a world forever shy of his expectations of it. Connor remembered that disarming feeling from years earlier, the ache of something molten inside he would spend years trying to bury, that thing which gave a sad, disembodied quality even to his laughter.

—How are they looking for the body?

—Snow squalls have the west shore covered. They'll send out a Cormorant when it clears. The kid jumped somewhere over the game sanctuary so it could take a while to search the area.

—Bears will get him by then – Jan stood up from the bed and pulled back the edge of the ochre curtain. His pickup truck was parked directly outside; an unopened pine freshener hung from the rear-view. In the windshield's reflection, a V of geese zippered across the sky, then vanished where the eaves met the glass.

—One thing I've learned – Jan turned, scratching his bare shoulder – is that forgetting something isn't any easier when you keep thinking about it. Don't beat yourself up, hear me? Anyway,

I've got to head out. A jeep's ditched up on Pine Lake. I told dispatch I'd take it.

—Suit yourself – Connor said.

He watched Jan get dressed. The dim margarine light of the motel room made Jan's body look younger. He was still boyish and lean where it counted but his face betrayed his age and heavy smoking. He buttoned his jeans over his crotch and slid the belt through its buckle. His chestnut pubic hair flashed through his fly as he did it up.

—I know it's not polite to say… – Jan put on his coat, the fur of the collar circling his face – but lots of those native kids have serious kinds of problems. I don't blame them for thinking up crazy ways to off themselves. It's not the kid's fault either, but you've got to be a little nuts to do it that way – Jan crossed the room and stood in front of Connor – I'll go and come back if you're still around.

—I don't take off until the morning. Maybe I'll just nap. Come by when you're done.

—Sleep well, handsome.

—Wear your seat belt.

Connor stood at the window warming his feet against the baseboard heater as Jan's truck pulled back onto the snow-packed highway. Jan's kiss dissolved on his lips in a memory of wet pressure.

—He's forgot to clip his chain – Connor thought. The chain of the tow swung from the winch like a sail main loose from its rigging – He'll get fined if a cruiser sees him. Not likely though. Not up here.

According to airline protocol, he was supposed to be sleeping in preparation for his return flight to Winnipeg the next morning. He'd insisted he didn't need stress leave but nonetheless he was kept awake by the image in his mind of the native boy lingering at the door of the plane. The wind at that altitude had been so cold he was certain he'd have ended up with frostbite if Terry hadn't ordered him back into the cockpit. But the kid had stood there, the brown skin on his arms goose-bumped, nearly white, the look on his face as though it had only been some May afternoon.

▲ ▲ ▲

Horizon to horizon across the domed expanse of sky, the contrails left by the aircraft would last for an hour at most, gradually fattening outward into a uniform haze fine as gauze. They would hover in the sunset, tangling with the treetops and hydro pylons, their bellies singed red and purple.

—More of them than usual – Jan thought, as the truck crested the hill at the Pine Lake turnoff. It was awesome to think how many people were in the air circling the globe, how many of us flew to where we could never get to by land. The vapor trails came and went with the kind of regularity that contrasted with their transience.

The truck pitched and swayed over the dirt track, the rusty suspension releasing the chassis up over the potholes. He'd picked up a few jobs along this road in previous months. Mostly game hunters who'd returned from the bush to find their tires deflated by the cold. Every so often the eight-seater from Ijiraliq would fishtail into the ditch. The Inuit were hearty Christians and made the sixty-four-kilometre journey into Rankin every Sunday for the service. His last call from dispatch had relayed that the jeep he was driving to now wasn't local. It would be hard to tell what he was in for. Locals knew to keep watch out for the random herds of musk oxen and rogue polar bears. Those unfamiliar with the North could easily become distracted by the inferior state of the roads. He'd been first on the scene after a family of campers had T-boned a male ox last spring.

—I've also pulled a body, frozen solid, from the water – Jan boasted to Connor – Shit, I had to wrap my chain around the guy's middle and haul him out with all his fishing buddies looking on. The ice just hasn't held this season. In all, around fourteen huts have fallen through.

—Terry flew cargo down in the Antarctic – Connor said – You can land a plane on only eight feet of ice.

—I'm telling you, this melt's a strange one. Once it gets going, there's no stopping.

Connor hooked Jan around the waist, gripping his own forearms in a secure lock. The smell of cigarette on Jan's skin was comforting as a campfire.

—The bears can't hunt their usual territory. That's why they're wandering down.

—Bears wander regardless – Jan turned his head – Try putting a fence around nature.

—What happens if they're boxed in. They attack?

—Sure, if they're threatened. You corner any predator, he'll attack.

Connor was typical of the men Jan found himself involved with. They carried a hunk of iron around inside them that Jan felt useful trying to suss out and then repair like a surgeon removing a bullet. It never ended the way Jan believed it could but he made the best of a difficult situation. Rankin was small enough that he knew to take what he could get when he could get it.

Whenever Connor was in town, the two men met in the far room of the Siniktarvik Motel. The owner, an aging Inuit hunter named Anawak, stayed put in the souvenir shop attached to the reception. The shop was a depleted rack of postcards, an array of polar bear snow globes on a melamine shelf above a thawed-out ice cream freezer. Anawak's cataracts prevented him from seeing who came and went from the parking space at the far end. For years he'd only asked that Jan pay upfront.

Jan spotted the jeep in the ditch about a kilometre down the road – a dark rectangle tilted against the brightness of the snow. Though the ridge was slight, in the flatness any altitude meant an impressive view of the surrounding tundra. Jan could just make out the darkened figure propped against the vehicle, but the sight of something swinging in his side-view drew his attention from the road. He slowed the pickup and pulled to the side of the gravel.

▲ ▲ ▲

Not long after he'd met Jan, Connor thought he'd heard the sound of a truck down the lane and had convinced himself Jan had somehow driven down to Winnipeg to see him. Connor ran to the opening at the far end of the tunnel of leaves where the lane met the county road. The fence of poplars that bordered their property bent and rattled their leaves, just starting to yellow in the fading daylight. Somewhere out in the acres of forest that backed onto their yard, a wolf howled. It wasn't yet dusk so the sound signalled a kill – a coon or a rabbit, Connor thought, even an elk or one of the neighbour's unlucky pups that had wandered too far from its territory.

As the sound of the truck grew near, he'd felt his heart quicken. There was something about both of his worlds approaching each other, like alien planets on a near-miss collision course that gave him the same feeling he'd felt during flight school. The attack of pressure in his chest he'd wanted to rely on, what he saw and felt inside, not the attitude indicator or altimeter spiraling down in the cut-engine chaos of free-fall.

—It must be difficult living in a world of so many odours tacked onto tree trunks – Connor thought, as the district's garbage truck rumbled past – How easy to misplace yourself.

In the far corner of the yard near the row of pears and blackberry bushes, his son Riley bounced on the trampoline. He fell into a rhythm as Connor walked back to him that hinted at something constant.

—Dad, how sensitive is a girl's crotch? – Riley landed on his knees and sprang upward, back into the air.

—Not very.

—Not at all?

—I didn't say that. Why?

—Someone kicked Carla in the crotch at school. She came home early – Riley bent his knees when he landed to gain more height on the following bounce. His arms flew outward, his sock feet impacting the taut surface with padded thwacks that reverberated into the creaking springs.

—She wasn't really hurt but Mom still had to go pick her up. Is it the same as when a boy gets kicked?

—No, it's not the same – Connor said – Who told you that?

Riley landed hard and flew high into the air. For a moment the boy was perfectly framed against what was left of the blue day. His smile as he soared was less what Connor noticed than the vapor trail of the 747 arching across the purpling sky behind him.

▲ ▲ ▲

—What that fall must have felt like – Jan thought, circling around to the back of the truck. Twenty-three thousand feet of deafening noise, the stubborn, arctic air refusing to enter the boy's lungs. The surface of the earth below crisscrossed with snow-capped trees and the dark moraines of glacial till that had been carried down from the extending ice cap millennia earlier.

Jan fastened the hook of the metal hoist to the rig with the rusty clip. Attached, the winch line bowed with gravity from the top of the boom, a heavy sag that mirrored the curve of the cigarette foil he'd crumpled and tossed to the snow. It felt good to love someone as guarded as Connor. To engage the mechanics of having to open up for someone else to examine, to exhibit all the vulnerabilities that had taken him so long to pack inside himself. It seemed counterproductive, but his emotional distance was one of Connor's flaws he felt he benefitted from.

Jan knew about Riley and Connor's youngest, Carla. He'd seen the unnamed wife smiling awkwardly in the backgrounds of the photographs Connor had shown him when they'd first met in the motel. But it was never a question of needing more than that. The simpler things were kept, the easier it was. For both of them.

Lighting a smoke, Jan walked back along the side of the truck to the hood. The jeep below must have hit an ice patch coming down the hill and veered off as it tried to regain control. The driver was a dark stationary point against the snow a little to the right, and Jan couldn't tell if it was a man or a woman by the distance. He'd finish the smoke and then drive down to pull the truck free of the ditch. It wasn't much to offer the world, but this was a respectable service and it made him feel useful to offer something other people couldn't.

The dark point stood in the distance and suddenly reached out for the vehicle. Jan saw the point slip and fall, landing in the snow like a period dropping to the bottom of a phrase. It lay there for a moment, stunned perhaps, and then strangely it began to slide away from the car out onto the expanse of snow that reached out to the horizon.

—Is the guy crawling somewhere? - Jan thought, flicking the cigarette butt and squinting to focus on the vehicle.

The point suddenly grew a tail of red as it slid. Unlike the airplane's contrails that scarred the sky so precisely, this red one blotched and zagged across the ice as it drifted outward. It was then Jan saw the movement of the bear. Camouflaged perfectly against the brightness, its white bulk tugged the point away from the car, leaving a long red smear that grew in length as the animal pulled the body.

Without thinking, Jan yelled out at the creature. His voice broke the vacuum of the air around him in a holler that morphed into a cry, filling the gigantic space with the kind of electricity that follows a gunshot.

Jan could see the bear stop in its tracks, its invisible form drawn like a transparent ghost laid over the white snow background. Jan had seen enough of them hunting for seals on the slick ledges of icebergs to know what one of their muzzles looked like covered in blood. The chill of the outside didn't subside when Jan jumped behind the wheel and sped down the hill towards the vehicle.

▲　▲　▲

Connor's granddad had told him that in 1974, when Connor had been just two years old, an iceberg the size of a warehouse had drifted into the shallow waters of Rankin Inlet. Larger than any of the dwellings on shore, it parked in the bay for almost a half year, melting slowly, changing shape as elegantly as an ice sculpture at a wedding. The villagers who'd come down to the shore to study it soon noticed a thick gash streaked through the middle of it. They conversed in small groups on the pebble beach, the women wrapped in blankets, the men in rubber boots skipping stones out to hit it. The ripples that broke the iceberg's giant reflection in the cold, dark water of the inlet quickly soothed over and mended.

—They've found people in icebergs before – one of them guessed – Mammoth hunters frozen since the last ice age.

But the dark spot was too extensive to be a single human. It spread out on a diagonal across the whole thing, bisecting the turquoise and cobalt stress lines and disappearing beneath the black of the waterline.

A woman holding a baby guessed it might be the frozen remains of a polar bear, but another quickly dismissed that possibility since he was a hunter and knew the bears were eaten by their comrades when they died or else sunk to the ocean floor to be devoured by microbes. They would have to wait. As the daylight increased, the warm breeze licked at the mountain twenty sun-filled hours all summer long.

One of the older men first recognized it, the circular leaf roundel of the Royal Canadian Air Force. He confirmed with a few of his friends whose opinion he knew counted for something: The fuselage of a F4F Wildcat, completely intact but for the tip of the left wing.

The men pondered a while and then surmised that after running out of fuel the pilot had crashed onto an ice shelf sometime during the end of the war. After three decades of snow had compressed into ice, the chunk had broken off the shelf and floated the entire plane in its crystal case into Rankin. When the melt would allow, the villagers would drag the plane free of the ice and tow it to shore.

—Do you think the pilot froze too? – a child with a maroon scarf wondered.

—I hope there's something valuable inside – said another.

Connor remembered the story as being one that his grand-dad had enjoyed telling him time and again. As a kid, Connor couldn't get enough of it. He had pictured the iceberg in the moonlight as a towering black void with a tail fin. Once, he'd even dreamt he'd swum out, climbed to the top of it and stared at the pilot's pale, frozen face. He'd woken and wondered what other gifts might be delivered by icebergs.

▲　▲　▲

Connor dried his hair and then the mirror with the motel's bleach-roughened towel. There was something about the look of the man staring back at him in the fog-wiped reflection that made him move the fingers of his right hand to his mouth and chew their nails to the quick. He hated the habit but it did something to soften the purr of anxiety that had started in the pit of his gut since Jan had called him from the police station. Jan's pickup was just pulling into the space in front of the motel room when Connor finally left the bath-room. He pulled on his boxers and huddled behind the door out of the cold as Jan stepped in. His lips were drawn into his mouth and he brought his cigarette inside without a second thought.

—The police said they would try to follow the trail – Jan said – but the males move quickly. There's no use going out to hunt for the body.

Jan stood with the smoking cigarette down at his side. He felt strange suddenly being indoors now, a sense of confinement that began to work its way across his body like the surface of a lake whose water was beginning to freeze.

—That's a really shitty thing – Connor said – Do you want to go out and grab a beer or something? Do you want to sit?

—Yeah, thanks – Jan took a drag from his smoke and sat on the edge of the mattress – I mean, I've heard of them getting at people before. Just didn't think I'd see it.

Still holding his damp towel, Connor sat on the bed beside Jan. It made Connor uncomfortable watching another man in the moments following something like this. Selfishly, it was more that he didn't like how he looked trying to comfort someone than it was that the other was suffering. Those were the parts of people Connor didn't really care to know about and he stared in silence at bed sheets and their pairs of legs lined up in a row. His bare thighs were the kind of pale that reminded him of when he was a boy and at summer's end his crotch would be white in the shape of his swim trunks. He imagined the polar bear's jaw clamping onto the leg's large muscle, tearing off a chunk with a sudden twist of its massive head.

—You destroyed your fingers – Jan said – What were you aiming for? Bone?

—Must have been - Connor studied the nubs of his nails - Just an old habit rearing. Do you feel better at least? It's a wake-up, I guess. That's what hits you most.

—I saw it from the hill - Jan said - the thing eating the guy alive out there. And I was watching it while it happened, thinking it was something different.

—You did what you could so don't feel bad. Take a shower if you want - Connor wrapped his arm around Jan, pulling his body closer - I'll join you in a minute if you want me to take your mind off it.

Although Connor wanted the normal, impish Jan back, the perturbed look in the man's eyes sparked something inside Connor as close to the pain of love as he'd ever felt. It was a feeling like red smithereens landing inside of him, hot iron. His hand rasped the whiskers on Jan's chin as he moved his face in to kiss him.

Jan's body tightened - Stop, I just need a moment...

—Come here then - Connor pulled Jan down to the bed.

The iron feeling had started to sear through him, a metal poker with a blazing orange tip. It was as though he'd been encased in ice his entire life and whatever was inside him had melted through it, exposing its nerve to the air.

—Give it a break - Jan said - Not now. I said I need a minute.

Connor felt the force of Jan's hands push back against his shoulders but the burning feeling wouldn't let him stop finding contact with Jan's skin.

—...Christ, Connor - Jan growled.

Connor moved his body on top of Jan's, pinning him to the bed with the force of his kisses. The more contact he made, the less painful the iron felt. Touching Jan felt like relief, like ice pressed on a burn. His fingers felt around Jan's crotch for the fly of his pants.

Jan suddenly brought the cap of his knee into impact with Connor's groin, a collision that felt soft and solid at the same time. The other man's reaction began as a sharp intake of air that changed into a series of whimpering moans as Connor rolled his body off him and curled at the corner of the bed.

That love could feel as sickening as a kick in the crotch, as a breath that refused to pull its way down into the lungs, was the newest of the sensations Connor lay there trying to make sense of. He opened his eyes again when he felt the blast of cold hit his face, in time to see Jan's silhouette pause at the open door of the room.

—I'm sorry - Jan said - Man, I'm sorry.

And in a moment, he was gone.

THE VAGRANT BORDERS
OF KASHMIR

Diesel fumes spin from exhaust pipes, vaporous tails in the hot morning air. Autos weave past on the street below already lifting sharp odours of cabbage, market peels, baskets woven from wet grasses. Blistering sun pulls sweat to my forehead, that feeling of being lost I always tried for as a kid and only finally succeeded at. Veneer of sand blown from the beach spread over asphalt. Through the palm trees the ocean rolls, spraying salt into the whole nostril mix of things.

Panaji Hotel rooftop waiting for breakfast with Ari.

Goa.

Ari leans over the concrete railing, peers down at the growling traffic. Shoulders brown as the milk coffee at my lips, tan still glistening with edges of red from yesterday's hike to the hill temple. Climbed together in the heat of the day with one water bottle to share until the top, sweat that dripped from his upper lip onto the plastic opening, handing it to me. Now standing beside a nest of electrical wires pinned to the corner of the building, he says – An army truck down there's unloading bags of onions – turns to the table – What are your plans after this?

—Probably head to some smaller beaches for a while. Couple of months maybe. Then Mumbai, Jodhpur, Agra, Kathmandu. Tibet, if money doesn't run out.

—And Alexis?

—Don't know. I'll stay with her most likely. At least until she's better. You really have to go? Bonderam festival starts in a week. Shame not to go all together, we'd have fun for sure...

—No, Cam. Can't do that. Manobhava is only initiating disciples for another three days. If I leave tonight, I can just make it to Jaipur in time. A train from here to Mumbai, Mumbai to Bhopal, and should be a few hours to spare when I get to Jaipur.

—And if anything goes wrong?

—I've got to try, Cam. You know this is important to me.

Alexis' room smells rusty like sick. Daylight filters between cracks in the orange curtains, dusty air-con sitting broken on the window ledge, her in a dirty white tank top sprawled on the mattress, breathing at least. Wooden door to the bathroom is open so walk across the cool tile, check if her water bucket is empty.

Whisper – I'm going to the end of the hall to fill your bucket. Do you want me to bring you anything? – thinking, *damn this is bad timing*, and her so afraid to drink the sadhu's water in the first place, believing it was full of parasites. Had said – This is a really shit idea, Cam. Look at the water. I don't care if he's holy or not – then the sadhu dipping his cup into the basin, holding it out first to Ari, then me, then a family of Indians as we waited for Alexis to decide. The sadhu's dark eyes and beard, loincloth, painted red forehead and Ari looking at him like he was really incarnate, with that full open stare like he wanted to put himself inside the sadhu's body to feel what it was like to actually live that other person, saying as he watched – What little we can get away with. A cup, a bowl, a stick of incense... *Namaste* – Always that guess inside making you wonder – *what if I just left it all?* – if I abandoned myself, joined that bony sadhu on his mat to meditate until the monsoon, gathered my things like a turtle and camped for ten years in solitude beneath the nearest sandalwood tree? Knowing that's the better choice, but that catch: a barb on a catheter.

Fill bucket from the faucet at end of the hallway, window open out onto the street with sacks of onions being unloaded. Tiny lizard – a soft translucent comma above the tap – then a Sikh man with blue turban stepping out of his room with his bucket. Smell of his oily beard in the heat, like wet coins, wet cardboard. Don't know if I could convince Ari to stay, with the time it takes to get to Jaipur and him feeling all fervently reborn since meeting one of Manobhava's disciples on Miramar beach, a French kid named Gilles whose eyes had said anything but trust me. Alexis and I swimming in the tumble-brown surf while the cattle chewed their cud under the palm trees, Ari standing waist-deep in the shallows with the French kid, saying – This is so interesting, because I've been hoping to find someone who knew a guru. Manobhava, you say, is a good teacher? I'm looking for someone with deep integrity, an open soul... – like a wound or a jar, I wondered. Open shifts into various forms.

Sikh man tilts his enormous beard at the tap, me walking back to Alexis' room with full, sloshing bucket. Don't know if I blame the sadhu entirely, Ari and I both fine after drinking his sanctified water. The mind projects what we already believe. Then her telling that awful news about her failed attempt and Ari saying – Now, that's what I'd have done. Nothing like bumming through India to help you forget your own misery – And Alexis with that look of wanting to say, *shut up, you can't possibly know anything about it*, so I said – Just the next thing. After something like that, just have to do the next, normal thing – That was in Varca where we first met, Alexis' hair in tattered red dreads, pupils black and open, and the sense that she had wandered away from something horrible and was trying her hardest not to remember where it was.

Ari puts on sunglasses – That French kid, Gilles. Such a young guy but he knew so much. It's amazing! He went to Manobhava's ashram in Jaipur at seventeen, left his whole life back in France and said he never looked back.

—Is that what he did.

—I'm serious, Cam. If he can do it, why shouldn't we? You and I both know this is how we should live. It's just a matter of finding the balls to take the first step.

Thinking, *that's fine for you to say*, then suddenly being hit with such a surge of jealousy that I look away because I know what this is all about, and then with the nerve to talk of finding the balls. *That's fine for you to say.*

Indian man, slim with black moustache, brings breakfast plates and sets them on the table. Bead of sweat polishes his jaw on its way down from his brown temple; hesitant smile apologizes for bad English – Okay everything, sir?

Then Ari says he wants another cup of coffee and the man backing away from the table like he's been told by his boss this is how you serve them, no matter what they ask for.

—See that? That's the problem right there! We've captured him. I'd get my own goddamn coffee but these structures are in place to prevent me from doing it. I'm talking about leaving all this behind. Manobhava's teachings will take us this direction. I want you to come, Cam. Why not come?

—What about Alexis?

—I don't know why you take such responsibility for her. Honestly, Cam, she'll be alright. India is full of sick people. Shitty thing, though I'd have run the same way if I was her. But this is about something bigger, Cam. It's a question of priorities.

Priorities. That widening tower built too fragile at the base, tapering outward into a precipice, vertigo, adrenaline of overhang, threatening crack.

—It's what you do when someone's sick, Ari. Would be the same for you. But I'm happy for you, I'm sure Manobhava's what you're looking for.

Man with moustache sets coffee on the table.

—Well, anyways – slips feet out of his sandals – There's no convincing me otherwise. I'm leaving for Jaipur tonight.

Our bare feet on the concrete nearly touching, rumble of army truck below on the street, that constant friction where our insides meet weather, senses, chances to abandon for good our lives boxed up in storage rooms, everything planned on going back to, vanished.

Not vanished. *Deserted.*

—How long are you planning to stay there?

—A year. Maybe two. I don't know. There's no point staying for less than that. Transforming yourself the way Manobhava teaches isn't some spectator sport. I know how much you like to dip your feet in to gauge the temperature.

—You can't blame me for being cautious.

—That's it! That's your weakness, you finally admit it. As much as I admire you for everything else, you're too damn cautious.

Precipice. Flailing hooves grasp for purchase on the crumbling rock edge, whole herds falling through mid-air. A shower of wool sprays over the cliff side.

Water bucket back to Alexis' room, her meager body curled beneath the mosquito net, condensation slinking down the sides of a water bottle into rings. From the doorway, smell of sick, stale heat of a dark room at noon. Women from the market outside sold all the goods from their tables and now load empty baskets onto carts attached to donkeys, morning earnings tucked away safely in the blouses of their saris. Over a billion scrounging daily while a humid breeze creeps along a dirty, paint-chipped windowpane down to the sweat line where it releases its coolness.

—Cam? – Alexis' dry-throated murmur – Can you get my sheet? It slipped off the end of the bed.

—Yeah. Filled your bucket too.

—I haven't felt this horrible since I left to come here. It was a mistake to trust that sadhu.

—Ari and I are fine, though. It couldn't have been him. Must have picked up something else.

—No. That's not how these places are. He was there to steal our money and you and Ari walked me right into it. You've always kidded yourself that way. Especially with Ari. But that's how we survive, I guess. That's how we get away with standing in the middle of this huge pile of shit thinking we're completely safe when we're not. No one is and that's the goddamned rule.

Sikh man passes the open door, glancing with turbaned head into the room. Pauses with bucket then continues down the hallway.

—Ask him if he has a cigarette.

—I'll come back later to check on you.

—Ask him for a cigarette, Cam. I'll share the smoke with you.

—Do you want food?

—Oh, just fuck off then.

Shutting the door, fresh breeze of the hallway. But her face, clamped teeth of devastation like a bear trap. Can't say what I would do in similar circumstance, surviving your suicide and your own father finding you in a bathtub of blood, but would certainly drop the floor out from under you – that damned eternal precipice, wide eyes, teeth tongue teeth, rabid frothing lips. Can't say what I'd do or who I'd blame. Alexis telling Ari and I the whole story at the guesthouse in Varca, me thinking –

That's fine, we all travel for different reasons – Isn't always with obvious purpose but everyone comes to India for one reason or another perspective. Maybe just to jump the fissure and for God's sake, what's wrong with fleeing if it saves you?

Ari, glancing at the clock on the inside wall, says – The train doesn't leave for another four hours. You could change your mind. I want to give you that option.

Say – That's fine. But I don't want to leave Alexis alone with all that to deal with.

—There you go, being cautious again, Cam. I hate to think what'll happen if you don't start saying fuck it. The deep end is shallower than you think. But hey, that's your decision to make.

Dark eyelashes, hint of Spaniard slouched in his plastic chair looking over his bronzed shoulder towards the railing. That envious leanness to his movements, like a man being trained to fight or jump hurdles. Tough gristle of sinew snagged between dogs' teeth, thigh bone clamped in salivating jaws.

In Varca: Alexis, Ari and I in the guesthouse restaurant overlooking the beach. Three beers sweat their rings onto the plastic tablecloth, TV in the corner of the ceiling reporting a family of Christian missionaries burned alive in their car by Hindus in the eastern state of Orissa. Motive cited as force-fully trying to convert the poor. Quick smack over the sucking fuselage of a horse fly. Note: Desire to eradicate our annoy-ances, dreams of peace without the bother, cremation fires lick-ing through the tough-skinned corpses of obstinacy. How a handkerchief over the nose easily blocks the acrid smoke of burning rubber, burning flesh.

Ari looks away – So simple just to demolish your misery, isn't it? Just put your neck through the noose and pull tight.

Or crash the car, he means, swallow pills, aim the barrel, slice the skin.

Alexis, wide-eyed, says – I'd dare you to try. Takes more guts than you've got – then pulls up the sleeves of her cotton shirt revealing without warning the still-red intersections on her wrists, as if to say *don't underestimate the balls it takes to end it.*

Ari saying – Now, that's what I'd have done. Nothing like tramping through India to help you forget your own misery – But Alexis with that look of wanting to say *shut up, you can't possibly know anything about it* and Ari and I wondering why or how or if anyone knew she was here or if she ought to be. Said she left Toronto a day out of hospital, flew into Delhi, hitchhiked with two Australians to Agra, Kanpur, Varanasi, but said the food sat strangely in her stomach and, besides, she didn't like the feeling north Indian men gave her. Dirty auburn hair matted back in salted dreads, angular face with sly nose, cigarette dangling from lips as she bends to rip loose the threads unravelling her skirt. Then wondering what torrent of desperation had carried her to the brink then pooled there as she surveyed her dismal hellscape then swept her over from behind. And why, as she was falling, didn't her arms suddenly flail and grab hold of a tree root, crumbling overhang and wrists trailing blood down to her elbows, not pulling with last strength back over the ledge?

—I don't know what possessed her – Ari says as the rickshaw weaves through dusty traffic from Panaji out to Maruti temple, the driver chewing betel nut, red saliva filling the sacks of his cheeks then spouting from his mouth a thick splatter onto hot pavement – I'm sorry, Cam, but I just don't understand it. What drives a person to that?

—Probably wanted to break free of her container – then thinking why all this to enclose us in the first place? Why so many walls and edges, damned precipice you either fall over or turn back at?

Then him looking at me, long with deep, sunned face, unshaven black scruff of the subcontinent traveller – Cam, I don't live by those rules. You see the way the men hold hands here? We'd think little or nothing about such preferences if our society simply ignored them. You're too damn careful. I hate to think where that prevents you from going.

Rickshaw halts by the base of the hill. Sun hits the dry stone in full glare and blaze, earth strewn with yellow boulders, mix of shrubs, clump grasses, heat and distant knock of cowbells. Two boys crouch in the ditch and catch crickets by hand, hold them up to their noses, then release them back into grass. Maruti temple perched high on the hilltop with a granite trail winding upward and behind, a lone sadhu cross-legged beneath an overhang. Climbing in the noontime heat, wondering about Alexis and how many of us stare out over the rims of escarpments onto weaving river valleys below, haze of smoke, exhaust, precarious footholds, whatever it is that keeps us from vaulting over.

Ari stops beside a boulder, looks at me, then drinks from the water bottle. Beads of sweat on his upper lip collide with the plastic opening, rhythmic gulps of his Adam's apple, glint of his saliva as he passes the bottle to me.

I say – I want to get to the top before long. Let's not lose momentum or there'll be no place to go when the sun is down.

Late afternoon light filtered dark through closed curtains. Mosquito net pulled to one side of the bed, Alexis sprawled, bottom sheet tangled around her feet like a collapsed shadow, revealing the dirty mattress.

—Cam? – pale voice from the pillow – Cam, I feel so horrible. I shouldn't have come here. I brought all my miserable shit with me, just clung to everything, Christ. Did you bring a cig?

—No.

—Has Ari left?

—Not until evening. His train leaves at six, I could tell him to come say goodbye, he's only up on the roof.

—Don't do that – then the gentle hush of footsteps in the hallway, the Sikh on his way to the water tap – Has Ari said anything to you?

—About Manobhava? He's convinced it's what he's supposed to do. He's asked me to go with him but I didn't think you could manage...

—Not about that – Alexis pauses under the distant rumble of an army truck, bringing hand to her forehead, wipes sweat, eyes half-hidden behind fissured wrists – I slept with him, Cam. I didn't know if I should tell you.

Crack.

Instant in mid-air when all four appendages thrash at sky, cantilevered cliff side pulls away, neck muscles taught with impending skull smash. Ten seconds of free fall, that mountain range rising from haze, heat of the rain-starved plains and city exhaust smogging the distance all the way from Panaji to Pune, Mumbai, Silvassa, Ahmadabad, Jaipur, Delhi, then north to the Himalayas, the vagrant borders of Kashmir.

—When? - I ask.

—The night we all first met in Varca. I went to his room when you left and he told me to come in. He must've felt sorry for me, I don't know. I shouldn't have told you but I thought it's better you know. You don't hide that sort of thing from a friend.

Windowsill vibrates the dead carriage of a horse fly, brittle paint chips, dust-drift, army truck emptied of onions pulls away into the swell of Panaji.

—You think you have a right to be upset, Cam?

—I'm not upset...

—Because it's times like this... - she says - when you're the loneliest, when you've exhausted all your other options...that nothing at all really feels like the better option. Goddammit, I shouldn't have come here. I know that now. There were a million things I could have done but I came thinking somehow the heat and the mess would distract me. And now being alone in this room for hours and hours...as bad as it was before, this is worse. I know he means something to you, Cam, but he felt sorry for me, I'm sure that's why he did it. It meant something to me too, just to have that body. And it means something that I can tell you...

—I'll come back to check on you. I'll tell Ari you're feeling better. He'd be happy to know that.

—Jesus, Cam. I just thought I should tell you before he left. Bring me some water when you come back. And for Christ's sake, find me a cigarette.

Condensation maps highways down the plastic bottle, Ari lifting his shirt, wiping forehead sweat. His taught abdomen, a line of black hair from his navel until waistband. Behind his head in a breezeless sky, two black pinpoints circling, their hawk-eyes spotting field mice. Ari says – We'll be back before it's dark. Not to worry – then put my lips to the mouth of the bottle, wet of his saliva, that constant sun and the feeling that sooner or later all of our subterrains eventually bubble to the surface, and why not here in India where it's easy to get lost and change forms? Hand the bottle back and watch him drink a second time – *There.*

An hour of climbing later, arriving at Maruti temple with a view stretching out over the boiling plains, the sprawled smudge of Panaji then the whole vast linear ocean in the distance, all those hidden troughs and ridges that tower beneath the water in submerged marine continents. Us on the stone railing that perimeters the temple, legs dangling above scrub weeds, a child tapping our shoulders, holding marigold garlands with one hand, and the bells from the temple in the background. Priest wakes the monkey god Maruti from his sleep and gathers handfuls of herbs from the glacial streams that spill from inside icy Himalayan crests, faithful devotee of Rama, kind simian of loyalty and thunderbolt. Boy with marigolds lingers behind the shade line, shadow from the roof cutting across his bare feet, brilliant loops of tangerine over his arms, then turning away, ducks inside the temple bordered by tall grass. Ari looks at me, smiles, moves his knee until it rests against mine.

Says – What little we need, don't you think, Cam? Isn't this what it all boils down to? Just two simple creatures, happy in their circumstances, contented apes with their arms around each other, surveying the jungle?

—How you put things – I say – makes me think there's something meaningful under all this mess. I'm glad you brought that water bottle. It's difficult to think ahead sometimes. I don't mean you can never not plan for things. But during the day, with the heat...

—Come to Jaipur with me... – then his quick kiss on my cheek, soft as bread mellowed in milk at the bottom of a bowl. Toes slip over the threshold, swift skid down the slope into scrubland, pebbles ricochet off fibrous plant stems, avalanche of crumbling dirt, torn roots and foliage – Let's go to Manobhava, Cam. Vanish together.

Together. Like a split shadow retracting into a common core, snake tongue moist with information coiling back into scaly mouth, glazed eyeballs, dragging tail with rattle: A smooth, vulnerable belly.

Then leaving Alexis' room with the slick crash of everything finally shuddering into position, shards of venomous metal lodged in the pink esophageal tunnel, palm trunk rubbed raw scabbing over with thicker bark. That aching chain and leg iron, that motorcycle roar like suddenly flying over the handlebars into a wire fence strung with barbs. Peel away, quivering wedges of flesh left dangling. Short pause before blood, urge to vomit, then choke, then sob.

—You are taking such good care of your wife – Sikh man in the hallway, grey beard tumbling over his face like the waters of a river rapid. Eyes I'd normally avoid but now feel like a deep well, brimmed with salve and calm.

—No – and then – I don't even know her really. I filled her bucket, that's all. She can take care of herself. I'm leaving tonight...

—May I ask how you enjoyed Goa? Beach parties are so popular with the tourists. Did you come for beach parties?

—No.

—If you came to see a guru, you should really go to Jaipur. Jaipur is most famous for its gurus, you see.

—I didn't come for that either.

Smile curls beneath his beard – Tourists only come to India for two things, either parties or gurus. Am I right? But then I am something of a tourist myself. I am from Kashmir, north of the Punjab. I've come to Goa on business as a seller of pharmaceuticals. Have you ever been to Kashmir? – Thick fingers comb, gather wisps at the base of his turban, twist and tuck back inside – It is the most volatile and beautiful place in the whole country. Our borders change constantly so the Punjab people are scattered everywhere throughout India. Such a phenomenon, don't you think? How people place themselves in this world?

—*Are placed* – I think. Borders have a tendency to rake and gather.

Then that lizard on the wall behind his head poised with suction feet, droplets from the faucet down water bottle, upper lip, jawline. The slow, tenacious force of liquid traversing surfaces, dangling from edges, held suspended by an eternal fidelity to identical molecules.

Then feel myself move closer to him, seeing the pores on his cheeks like divots in a full brown moon, ferocious grey beard, and me not certain of anything except a scalding loneliness that creeps up from my belly into the cave of my mouth, burns at my teeth and then suddenly pours out in a cascade of hot, violent sobs – a mustang leaping wild against his paddock. Strong and muscular, his arms gather around me as I give in, resting against the warmth of his skin through cotton shirt, smell of curry heated through sweat, faint cologne like wood chips and mineral. My frantic breaths through scattered weeping, the Sikh's hands on my back pulling me into his shoulder. From inside his chest, I hear him offer a deep bass of soothing moans, empathetic, the nook of his neck taking my tears as he rubs full-palmed against my skeleton. Then, in my feeling like a fragile cloud just spent of its thunder, he takes my shoulders and holds me away from him.

—I hope you manage to get to Kashmir someday – he says, dropping his blue-turbaned head in a conscious bow – It is really the most beautiful of places on earth. I sincerely wish you that pleasure – he turns and disappears into his room.

Then down the hallway to mine where I gather my belongings from a water-marked table, the lighter rings where the varnish disintegrated. Passport, handkerchief, Aspirin, guidebook. Backpack with T-shirts, sandals, plaid longyi I huddled beneath in the rocking carriage of the night train from Bangalore weeks before. Dim mounded bodies three-tiered under cabin lights and ceiling fans, an Indian man reading his Bible by penlight curled on the middle bunk. Crossing the Western Ghats with the pole star glowing out the open window, humid night breeze wipes across foreheads, the passing lights of the countryside. Zip pockets, hoist bag on back, glance beneath the sagging bed frame for the plastic bottle cap I dropped last night but never found. Leaving Goa. Away from Alexis. From Ari. From that curse of water bottles, accidental knee-touch, hallucinated kiss on the cheek meant to capture me. Forget them. Thirteen hour night-bus north, to Varanasi instead where troops of monkeys perch on temple rooftops, the promise of sunrise over cleaner rivers. Flatter, more forthright ground. Dreams of peace without the bother. White mineral deposits, bubbling subterrains, a glistening wet trickle over snow-dusted rock faces, storm-front cirrus, oxygen, the cobalt blue sky over wild and treacherous borders.

FROM THE LOOKOUT THERE ARE TREES

The power is out for the fifth night in a row, the moon still half-hidden beneath gnarls of black gas – truck exhaust blown upward. Beyond the deck of the guesthouse, the indigo shadow of a satellite dish swivels towards that glowing moon like a giant phototropic leaf anchored to the building's roof. Behind it, the golden stupa in the centre of Kalaw suddenly illuminates; the monks must have ignited the generators. The chugging thrust of combustion echoes out over the town as dogs with clicking paws sniff the pavement, foraging for food on the street below. My stomach growls, mixing with the engine whirr: All creatures wanting to eat tonight, that's the scavenger in us. So I grab a vest and cap, pick burrs from my bootlaces caught from yesterday's trek to the lookout; I lock the door to my room and head out into the blackened street.

Nighttime village. Kalaw. The foothills of the Himalayas.

▲ ▲ ▲

The bus grinds to a halt under a flank of fluorescent bulbs. The driver's naked voice shouts back to us, all sleep-quieted and still. The aisle lights flicker on and we creak open like moist shells from our bundles of sleep. Passing through Naypyidaw means government checkpoints, the army's paranoia manifested as a constant pain-in-the-ass. I search for my sandals kicked off in the grit beneath the seat, grab my jacket and yawn with the woken others. Off the bus onto the roadside ledges of Burma.

Heavy-eyed passengers shuffle through the midnight hut, the patrolmen inspecting identity cards and flashlighting faces.

—*Foreigner! Hello, foreigner* – a lone soldier gestures me away from the queue to the road – *You come here. Yes, come here, foreigner!*

His rifle cuts a shadow across his cheek.

—*Where is your passport?*

—Here. Canadian.

—*You travel only one, foreigner?*

—Yes, alone.

—*Alone...Alone. You have no friends.*

—I have friends.

—*But they don't come with you.*

—Not to Myanmar.

Over the guard's shoulder the empty highway to Naypyidaw blazes like a spotlit inferno. Clean black asphalt, five deserted lanes in either direction, properly curbed and garden-lined. The army has their own private road network so they don't have to drive with the masses. Same reason they won't allow monks to speak with foreigners at the Shwedagon. Coward paranoid bullshit.

—*You go to Mandalay?*

—Kalaw.

—*Kalaw for trekking?*

—Yes. For trekking.

—*How you like it, here in Myanmar?*

—It's fine.

—*Why your friends not come with you?* – he hands me my passport.

—They stayed in Thailand.

—*Thailand, no good. See? You come to Myanmar.*

—Myanmar's not perfect.

—*Not perfect, no. Go that way, your bus. Foreigner, goodbye.*

Back in my seat, a pock-faced soldier paces down the aisle sniffing for contraband and stowaways. Out the window beside the patrol hut more soldiers wrapped in blankets and knitted hats sit smoking cheroots and shuffling sticks into smoldering fires. A rash of embers pops into the air. During nights like these, awoken in the roadside gap, the in-between of destinations where the fields stretch out into a fathomless black and the humans wear all the weary lines their faces can bear, I ask myself where on earth I am and why in the world I brought myself here. Countries later, I still find myself forgetting.

The bus revs its engine and soon we're rumbling down the decrepit two-lane highway again. In the distance, the lights of Naypyidaw stretch out across the fields. Even at three a.m.

everything is lit like daytime. Across the aisle, two British guys have put on their sweatshirts and contorted their bodies into some sleep-bearable position. The air-conditioning has everyone huddled into themselves but no one wants to say to the driver we're damn near freezing. I tuck my knees up to my chest as that pit of hunger suddenly expands into a cavern of empty. Can't do anything about it now. Not until a rest stop at least. Thirteen hours north from Yangon to Kalaw.

▲ ▲ ▲

The headlights of cargo trucks shoot through the chilly night in beams that curdle the retina closed when stared at directly. The street dog beside me peers through the darkness, snout forward. Even that lagging hound so tiresomely using his stomach to slink through the black.

On the sidewalk a generator throbs in front of the small roadside restaurant. A fluorescent bulb dangles above the stove where a man ladles oil into a rusty pan, then the sizzle of onions. I ate at this place already for lunch but the fried rice is the best I've found so far. The tables look out onto the street and through the back window you can see the golden stupa when it's lit. I saw one of the British guys from the bus standing on the deck of the guesthouse when I left my room. He leaned against a wooden post surveying the darkened town and that gigantic satellite dish like he'd been pondering something dark and severe. Or maybe he was thinking of where to go next, since that's always what we're wondering. Where next? So happy to be nomads.

Plumes of steam from some wilted greens hit the cooking man in the face. As the restaurant owner looks up from the bar, his face brightens and says – You back already? Already today you eat here.

—Hungry again.

—Sit, sit. Okay. Same table you want?

—Doesn't matter.

—Again you eat fried rice?

—Sure – and then – Electricity's off again. Every night now, isn't it?

—Every night, sure. Every night. Sometime it stay on, but...you know. Not now. Maybe later.

—I'll have a beer too.

—One beer...

The owner is a young Burmese guy who somehow got his hands on a pair of worn Levi's and a black motorcycle jacket so he looks like an Asian James Dean. His wife sits at the corner table with the baby on her lap. She wipes the surfaces, brings the bill or a cigarette when the meal's finished, but usually just sits there playing with the kid or staring out at the golden stupa.

I say to him – Maybe it'll come back on.

—Football game is tonight. They give us electricity for that. The army always gives electricity for football.

Out on the sidewalk in front of the restaurant the two British guys from the guesthouse appear. One with dark shaggy hair coming down over his forehead. The other, blond, taller, with the most angular face I've ever seen, like carved by a torrent of mathematics.

The owner says to me – Please wait, please. Two more foreigners – and then goes to the door to seat them.

Foreigner. Foreigner. Come here, foreigner. Trespassing in that territory not your own: the riverbanks of lawless Burma, endless fields of slave-grown rice and knowledge of those vast hidden valleys of opium tucked away behind the mountain range, down roads no foreigner has the permit to travel.

▲ ▲ ▲

The vapor of my exhale coats the flashlight's beam, the temperature's dropped close to zero but I don't have the sweaters for it. I took the blankets off the empty bed and doubled them on top of my own. I froze my balls off in the bus from Yangon too. Everyone was bundled in caps and jacket-layers, glad for the respite from the heat, but I was just aching to roast. The tropics are for sweating out your toxin. It seeps out your pores and congeals into a scum you scrape off and rinse down the drain. But here the altitude is higher, Kalaw settled on the brink of the mountain chain before edging down to the Shan Plateau. The Himalayan foothills scuffing the Indo-Chinese peninsula.

Booted footsteps across the porch to the room next door: A Spanish couple returned from trekking today, come back from dinner and begin to play music from some iPod speakers. I hear them unpacking and repacking, their minutes of comfortable, mutual silence through the wall and then the guy's sudden off-tune singing. The girl joins in a quarter-pitch higher.

My flashlight fades to a sickly yellow. I knock it hard against my book cover and it flashes brighter, then weakens to the same jaundiced ray. The Spanish couple is silent again and I imagine them in the beginning strokes of a passionate kiss. The room is completely quiet as the flashlight fades its last beams into black. Cold and dark, huddled under these blankets alone: the ache of the solo traveller settles on top of me like some nighttime nausea – some cage I stare out of like a bus window onto the passing river valleys. The weight of solitary transport, the desolation of a second pair of eyes not there. I'd convinced myself it was better this way. Complete freedom without the bother, without the worry of someone else's stomach growling for food, their legs tiring from the pace, plus all the portals travelling alone would open. But now in this freezing dark, I feel like a remnant – lost and unmatchable. Behind the wall, the Spanish couple attempts to fuck quietly.

▲ ▲ ▲

The owner seats the British guys at a table next to mine in the centre of the room. They order beers, and when he comes back I order a cigarette.

—Sure, sure. One cigarette.

—The Londons are fine – I say – I'll take one of those.

—One London...

The guy with the angular face looks over as the owner brings me the smoke.

—You ordered just one?

—You can do that here – I say – Have a London, though. The local brand will knock you out.

—I've smoked them before.

The other one says – You're at the same guesthouse as us.

—I think so.

—Did you trek today?

—Yesterday.

—Alone?

—With a guide from the guesthouse.

—To the lookout?

—You're quite high at that point.

—The view was incredible.

—We're going to Inle tomorrow. Have you been?

—Everyone goes to Inle. I've heard Hsipaw is quieter.

—We've been there too. On the way in, a week ago.

—How long have you been here? – I ask.

The brown-haired guy answers – This is our third week in Burma. We came in from China.

—I didn't think you could do that.

—We teach English in Baoshan, just across the border.

—The Burmese have terrible pronunciation.

—Chinese are worse. Their tongues get lost in their own mouths, don't they, Jake.

The angular guy leans back in his chair – We get cheated so often because we're foreigners. That's how it goes, though. I don't mind it so much, but Seth always takes it personally.

—I don't really – the guy Seth says.

—I was followed in Yangon – I say – I'd rather be cheated than followed.

—But the Chinese will cheat you to your face.

—They think we can afford it. That's why.

—We were on the same bus as from Yangon, weren't we? – the one named Jake says.

—Yes, I saw you. We took the same truck to the bus station too. Everyone goes the same direction through here. It's hard to find a place to be alone – I stub the cigarette in the dish.

—Jake didn't think you spoke English.

The owner arrives at my table – One fried rice...

▲ ▲ ▲

The bus grumbles slowly along the side of the mountain, hovering in that insomnial space between first and second gear. Black plants coated with dust shake as we pass. Drifts of four a.m. cloud catch the headlights as we climb into cooler air, farther into Burma, farther north into Shan State where the opium grows. Why am I here? Why can't I sleep, and why always alone? The shaggy palm huts built right up against the road are coated in the same dust as the plants. They shroud some huddled family against the roadside chill. The guys across the aisle are attempting to sleep too. Keep seeing their heads nod then jerk back to awake when the angle bumps off. I think they're British but can't tell. I'll see them around the town or some village monastery tomorrow. That's how it works – the same travellers following the same well-worn paths. I lay my head against the cold pane of the rattling window and watch the anonymous huts pass, full of dozing babies, mothers, fathers, brothers gone missing for years and years.

Then along the ditch, blurred human shapes begin to flash by the periphery of my sleep-starved eyes. A line of them, spaced evenly like telephone poles but couldn't be: Men and women – their hands bound with chains, heads bowed, feet apart and ankles shackled. Their skin is dusted with the blow of the passing cargo trucks, longyis dirt-stained and torn. Dozens of them line the roadside like totems, a forest of deliberately planted trees.

—*Prisoners* – a voice whispers from the seat behind me, a man chewing segments of an orange – *Them prisoners by the army. You know...politics* – A fleck of orange catches his lip.

▲　▲　▲

The lights suddenly flicker on. Across the street, cheers and applause from men smoking at the tea shop, their seats already saved for the game. The television screen, no bigger than a book, hums to life and the flames of lighters ignite fresh cigarettes.

The owner goes out onto the street and switches off the generator. Then the restaurant is just the quiet silt of night air, quiet except for oil in the pan.

—Every evening now – I say – since I've been here.

—They deal with it well, though – says Jake.

—The army drains it all to Naypyidaw. They keep every road lit, even in the middle of the night.

—We heard there would be military on the way to the look-out. Is that true?

—On the far side of the valley there's a barracks. You can see it.

—We heard it was a college.

—You mean the one in Pagan.

—That's a horrible story... - Jake continues.

—Yes, but go on. You should tell him - Seth says.

—You know you can take a boat from Mandalay to Pagan...

—That's right.

—On our boat there were soldiers who were escorting a prisoner of some sort. They kept him in a cage on the deck.

—A prisoner of what?

—I don't know, but there were soldiers guarding him.

—There were two. And they had their rifles. He must have been political. They said they were transferring him to a prison in Pakokku. But it's a tourist boat, so there's all these backpack-ers around him. And an Austrian woman asked one of the sol-diers why they were taking him, what had he done.

—She had guts.

—Yes, and listen to this. We're sitting there, you know, wondering what this was all about. And then Seth here noticed the man was mumbling to himself.

—Mumbling what?

—He was saying something under his breath. We couldn't understand it at first. But then we started recognizing English words and then realized he was talking to us, but quietly so he wouldn't get caught. He was being forced to kneel so he couldn't look at us, but he was saying something about foreigners in Burma...

—That's right – Seth said – *Foreigners must know what's happening in Burma*. That's what he said...

—He was a professor.

—Right. From the University of Yangon.

—And there was an older French lady who took his picture and passed him food through the bars. She wanted to do something.

—Food?

—She only had some bananas.

—Some Germans tried to give him dollars when the guards weren't looking, but the prisoner said he couldn't take the dollars. Said dollars were useless to him in prison.

—He needed kyat.

—But then the guard spotted us and said we shouldn't give him money. We could give him food, but no money. He had a few thousand kyat tucked under his feet from the French couple but then the soldiers searched the cage and found it.

—They took it from him and told us we could only give him food.

—They spoke English?

—The guards didn't but we knew what they meant.

—The prisoner actually spoke very well, Seth thought so.

—The guards weren't happy his English was better than theirs.

—The man could talk to us and the guards couldn't understand, you see.

—They got angry and put a tarp over the cage.

—It was this big plastic sheet.

—The French couple was really moved. The woman was, wasn't she, Jake?

—She started crying when they covered the cage with the tarp. She couldn't help it.

—You couldn't say anything?

—The Germans tried. But the soldiers said it was their job.

—And the French woman was crying because she couldn't believe it. She said it wasn't fair and she couldn't bear it. We were stuck on the boat, you see…

—Yes – I say – I think so.

Then the angular guy's face locks at the doorway. All of us turn as a green-uniformed soldier steps into the restaurant, a slender woman in a longyi traipsing behind him. The patrons are quiet as the officer speaks to the owner then is seated near the far wall, the gazes of the other diners lowering to the plastic tablecloths printed with soccer balls. The officer has the darkened skin of someone who spends his time outdoors, probably in charge of a battalion or two. His forehead appears devoid of creases until it furrows when he looks our direction. The woman's face is a smug doll with tiny, bitten lips.

▲ ▲ ▲

The flashlight is completely dead now. I'd laid it somewhere on the bedding so when I rolled over it dropped to the floor with a cold, cylindrical thud. Hope the bulb didn't break. I'll buy new batteries tomorrow if the shops have them. Seth and Jake, both pleasant guys, hiking to Inle in the morning and starting early. My trek to the lookout was stunning. My guide Harry knew everything about the landscape, the bark of the trees, how the water buffalo follow precisely in each other's footsteps so they won't break their legs. He knew about the poppy farms near the Chinese border you could only get to by truck – four days into the mountains by road. Knew about how the traders smuggled opium in the rectums of cattle and how the army oversaw it all. We stayed the night at a farm on the lookout and could gaze down into the dusk-filled valley and hear the tea harvesters talking by their distant echoes, their tiny shapes shifting on the far surfaces of the slopes as they picked. The farm grew every kind of food – a sky-forest Eden in perpetual harvest: Squash vines, papayas, citrus, beanstalks, fields of snap peas, marigolds and roses. Goats and squadrons of chickens patrolled the yard. I took a shower using a bucket and cold water from a trough, naked and looking out over the valley as the sun set. Harry said that on a clear day you could see all the way to Mount Popa near Pagan. That's a hundred kilometres away, I said, and he said yes, but you can see it. A warm wool blanket and dinner waited for me inside the smoky hut and at night the stars pierced through the black canopy – a billion of them, like there were more of them than sky. And they had a depth too; not just a flat surface but a space you could actually see into, like you could tell which of the light had travelled from farthest away. Across the canopy of stars, a satellite drifted like a beacon, white and blinking, tracing the curve of space.

▲ ▲ ▲

The officer looks over at us, his thick lips cushioning a toothpick. He leans over and says – *You are American, no? Three Americans in Burma...*

—We're British – Jake says.

—Canadian – I say.

—*Americans...come to Burma...for trekking* – his ruddy face drops, drunk, as if searching the racks of his brain for some lost vocabulary. He calls over to the owner in Burmese and repeats his demand to him. The officer gestures to us.

Then the owner translates – He say, it very dangerous for everyone in Burma when the foreigner talk about politics...

—No – I say – We didn't talk about politics. We don't even care about it really.

—We came for the trekking – Jake says.

The owner translates back and then from the soldier to us again. His hand trembles beside the pocket of his Levi's.

—He wants to know where you stay. What guesthouse.

—Don't tell him that, Jake. He doesn't need to know.

The officer pushes his chair back from the table, keeping his eyes somehow on all three of us at once. The owner has that look on his face like he was going to be in for it if we didn't leave. Across the road, a ball is kicked into a net and the men at the tea shop jump up to applaud the TV.

—Again he ask – the owner mediates – You stay what guesthouse?

—Don't tell him – Seth says – It's none of his business…

—I won't. We'll leave, it's okay.

Seth and Jake stand from the table and reach for their wallets to pay. The wife in the corner lays the baby on the table and tallies the bill on the pad. But the officer puts his hand out, mutters to the woman with the tiny lips and they both stand ready to leave. The officer stares at the owner, a long dark glare the colour of a lie. He drags his index finger across his throat. The restaurant is a rectangle of silence as they turn and leave.

—We weren't even talking about politics – I say – Don't know what his problem was.

—He was listening to us, from outside…about the boat ride.

—I don't know.

—That must have been it.

Then the restaurant plunges back into darkness. Across the road, the men watching football cry out as the television snaps off. Moments of pitch black at the plastic-covered table, silent except for the shouts from the tea shop, then the sudden pull-start of the generator and the feeling that everything in the country had been kicked in the gut but was determined to get up again like it had a thousand times before.

▲ ▲ ▲

I say goodnight to the British guys and wish them luck on their trek. I close the door to my room and feel around for the flashlight in the dark, my room where my backpack lay open on the second bed looking in the shadows like the mound of a sleeping body I was finally coming home to. It was a shame the men across the street couldn't finish the game. Their dejected footsteps picked across the shattered sidewalks ahead of me, the beams of the oncoming headlights blinding us.

The Spanish couple is silent now. I curl beneath the blankets thinking about what Seth had told about the prisoner. That was tough to hear, especially after the officer left the restaurant having done what he did. I hope the owner is alright. But that's how these places are, I think, as I pull the blankets over my head. Beautiful but dangerous. The owner had to translate to us and I could see on his face he didn't want to but had no choice. All of us understood and were on his side. And then the frustrated shouts from the men across the street where the TV had gone out.

Maybe I should have stayed in Thailand, stayed swinging in hammocks next to beach bars, not venturing out into the wilds of Asia just to suffer this loneliness. Like at the lookout, when I stared across the valley feeling fresh after my shower and the water buffalo were called home by the bells of their owners as the sun set. The huts down in the valley beginning to smoke from their evening fires and the children chasing their dogs and the hills glowing purple in the dusk and beyond them, just the trees.

A FIRE IN THE CLEARING

Gravel ricocheted off the undercarriage as the steel-coloured Volvo sped up. The steady percussion of stones masked the noise of the camping gear shifting in the trunk as the vehicle pitched and swayed over potholes. The road getting worse meant he was nearly there. All his favorite places in the province were like that, at the distant ends of deteriorating gravel roads. He loved the kind that led to where you could drive no further, where you would slow to a crawl, become blocked by a body of white-capped water or an impassable forest of spruce, the kind that lead to the cabin.

The blue glow of the dashboard matched the headlights' intensity. A shower of insects blazed white on the windshield. As a boy he'd seen deer along this road – a doe had once darted out with her fawn. Their coal-black marmoreal stares froze in the high beams and for the only time he could remember he'd heard his father swear out loud.

Goddamn deer. Just in time.

This far north the lakes fanned outward like amoebas. Wild eskers of forested shoreline separated each inlet and cove, wending around each other in a geographical labyrinth. The radio still crackled with reception. He'd expected that much at least, but surprisingly his cellphone still showed three bars. Progress, sure.

A kilometre more, he thought.

He would assemble the tent using a fire for light. To gather wood he would have to be cautious and use the headlights. Running out of battery this deep in the backwoods could land him in all sorts of trouble he'd rather not think about. He'd get the flames going by nesting birch bark with clumps of old needles and dead leaves. Later he would add kindling, a few heavier branches. Larger blow-down would be easy to find and there was never much wind that would make it past the treeline at the shore. One dead pine or cedar would be fuel enough. It was good there wasn't any wind, he thought. There was also moisture on the grass and in the soil – just a few centimetres of peat over a bedrock of limestone, only enough for a thin set of roots to grow. Dry, peat soil could spread a fire, even keeping it alive underground if given a steady supply of oxygen.

When he pulled into the clearing and stopped, the grass came as high as the driver-side window. Through the rolled-down opening he smelled the damp stalks and the wet tannin of mud. He switched off the headlights and sat in silence as the familiar shape of the cabin began to edge itself out from the blackness. He breathed in full lungs of air in the audible quiet: crickets, a frog croaking its coordinates somewhere in the dark like a two-toned ratchet, the sound of waves muted in the distance.

Slowly the posts of the weathered grey porch appeared, then the tilted eaves of the roof stopping where the blackberry bushes had wildly overgrown. Next, he saw the worn log siding, the Indian chair crafted from bent saplings and bark. The faded colour in the corner was a forgotten beach towel, crumpled and solidified beneath ten winters of snow. The cabin looked smaller than he remembered. The roof had caved at the back, maybe that was why. He was always surprised at the difference the passing of years made to the memory of objects. Rooms shrank. Ceilings drifted downward. How much smaller everything was that had been magnificent and indestructible as a kid. So fallible what had once seemed faultless. Nothing ever stayed the same as you remembered it.

The cell phone vibrated on the front seat. Flipping it open, he stepped out and undid his fly, turning toward the forest.

—Hi – she said – Are you there?

—Yeah. Just now.

—What's it look like?

—Hasn't moved.

—So it's the same.

—Nearly. Roof's fallen in a bit.

—What's that noise?

—I'm taking a piss.

—Jesus...

—Long drive, hon.

Her receiver made a noise as it scuffed against her chin and then he heard a soft cuss word like her voice was far from the mouthpiece. He shouldered the phone and did up his fly.

—...I just stubbed my toe on the bed – she said.

—Sit down then. Stop pacing.

—So tonight? Will you?

—The morning's better. In the light.

—You promised, though.

—I know...I know I did.

Closing the phone, he was alone again in the quiet. Through breaks in the cloud he caught brief glimpses of stars. The clearing looked brighter; his eyes had better adjusted. Dim bursts of light flashed through the branches as the beam from the Knife Island lighthouse whipped around from the far side of the bay. As a boy he used to lie in bed in the loft, the plaid curtain pinned back from the window, counting the flashes before falling asleep. The sound of the evening news muffled upward from the radio where a lamp glowed beside the easy chair his father reclined in. If he snuck out of bed and picked silently across the floor, he could peer over the wooden railing at the mass of his father's hair, thick as bear fur, spiking over the headrest. Cans of meat stew still yawned open on the counter from dinner. *Get to bed*, his father scolded without turning. How can you tell, Dad? *I just can*. Maybe it was a raccoon. *You're a raccoon. Now get to bed.*

From where he stood in the clearing, he could see up to the tiny window and the plaid curtain he'd tacked back on the nail. So much had happened, he thought. Some time ago. Ages ago. The same cabin, the same log walls. His own childhood seemed so remotely impossible.

After the kindling caught fire, he brought a heavier log to lay on top the pile. He assembled the tent to one side of the fire and then crawled inside to lay out the sleeping bag. From inside, the fire was a soft, constant glow through the nylon. He soaked up the pleasure of the tent, its paper-thin membrane that could trick you into believing that whatever lurked outside it couldn't get you. His own daughter Alexis had loved camping for the same reason. It was the idea of protection, she confessed, more than anything.

Webs snagged his hair as he stepped onto the sagging porch and felt above the lintel for the key. He hadn't needed to lock it since there was nothing inside worth stealing. Vandals and thieves weren't even a minor threat up here. People were just accustomed to locking up their things. It made them feel safer having the key to something – worthless or important, it didn't matter. The lock resisted in his hand. He forced the key inside and had to use all his might to twist through its rust for it to open. When it finally gave with a *thwack*, he hesitated. What if everything were the same?

He felt like a burglar when the door creaked ajar and a ripple of light from the fire outside fell onto two dinner plates still vertical in the drying rack. The kettle on the stove was a frozen grey hen. Cutlery was scattered like rusted tools on the peeling laminate. Covered with dust, a cracked bar of soap still lay in its dish. As he stepped inside, the musk of the place pulled into his nostrils: Mold, soot, wet carpet with its watersnake smell, damp paper, sulfur, some tinge of metal like the aftertaste of eating snow. Breathing it all in, his eyes closed involuntarily.

Suddenly he was a boy and his father stood at the stove boiling water, his broad shoulders caped in the red lumberjack's coat that always hung behind the door. His dark terrifying beard, his thick hair pushed up at the back where the pillow had pressed. *You helping me make the coffee? Come here then. Measure carefully.* Can I have some too? *When it's ready, if you like.* The morning heat buzzed off the grasses outside, the whole clearing a hot August meadow. The sound of his father's boots on the floor, the steam from his first cup of coffee held cautiously in his hands.

As his father had been with him, he'd been as severe with Alexis. Daughters were gorgeous yet unpredictable as pastures. She'd spent the summers with him at the cabin as a girl trapping bullfrogs along the shore in crude rock paddocks while he chopped and stacked firewood. Her hair would turn bleached and matted with the sun, freckles spraying bright constellations across her nose. When the autumn arrived and the nights turned colder she'd never wanted to leave. But while in the hospital, she'd refused to even look at him. He stood beside her outside in the snow as the smoke from her cigarette bathed up over the bandages on her wrists, the frozen turquoise of her hospital gown, the plastic I.V. tubing that held her upright like the strings of a marionette, the fiery red of her dreadlocks. *You can't stop me, Dad. Not if you tried. I'm in charge of what happens to me. When will you get that? You haven't realized I'm not your daughter anymore.* Even his memories of her seemed to be turning colder.

The roof buckled critically over the small table his father had used as a desk. From the clearing he hadn't been able to tell, but from inside the whole back corner looked like a kicked-in cardboard box. Magazines were puffy with moisture. Rodents had shredded the newspapers. Cedar and pine needles blanketed most surfaces. *How can something endure such loneliness?* He wondered where he'd been, what tasks he'd been absorbed in elsewhere while the roof silently, gradually, caved in.

The sky through the roof beams brightened the room. From the opening a raccoon spied at him. Startled by the door, it perched guiltily out of reach. Behind him, the fire outside was centered in the doorway, a perfectly contained rectangle of light.

Still hanging on the nails that punctured the log siding, his father's hunting caps hung, limp and greasy. The old man once asked him to burn a stack of papers in the fireplace, so he'd gone and lifted the entire pile off the table. He squatted and fed them one by one into the fire: Old issues of *Canadian Geographic*, phone books, pharmacy prescription bags, grocery and hardware receipts, a few pages his father had scribbled on. He watched them curl into ashy feathers on top of the glowing logs. *Wait now…Stop. Did you take those pages too?* No. *The ones I was writing on?* Panic. No. Then the chair shoving backwards as his father stood up and the sound of his boots on the floor and the weight of his presence beside him as he stared silently for some time into the fireplace. I'll write them for you again, Dad. *No*, he paused. *A loss like that you don't make up for with something else...*

Outside, the fire popped. A rash of embers exploded into the air. The raccoon shook its coat in a huff of fur, stared back one last time and then disappeared onto the roof. Its paws made a sound on the tin that reminded him of being underwater in a river – pebbles tumbling and clacking against themselves, wearing off their edges.

His pocket vibrated again.

—It's me – she said.

—I know.

—Do you think you could do it tonight? I mean, would you?

—Just one night, hon. The tent's set up.

—Have you been inside yet?

—Yeah. The roof's a mess.

—I said it would be rotting. No one's used it in so long.

—I didn't think it'd been that long.

—So will you? – Her voice faded out and he could tell by its tone she was looking down.

—Alexis wouldn't have wanted this. She wouldn't have cared...

—No, not for her. Jesus Christ, it's for you!

—It won't change anything.

—It will!

—But how?

—You've just become so, I don't know... – silence filled the receiver – ...unbearable.

He stared at the empty fireplace, the ash heaped and spread like a litter box. Grey raccoon prints faded out across the floor.

—Have I?

Why the cabin? he'd asked her one night in bed, her back towards him smooth as a dawn lake, the pink curve of her hip that after twenty years still fit perfectly into his palm. What difference would it make now? Why more loss after so much already? *Because I don't want to resent you* – she'd said – *And because you need to know what it's like to lose something for good. On purpose. Forever.* You don't think I did? We both lost her. Alexis was ours. *It's not the same,* her hip rolled from his hand. *I mean, stop trying to save her and lose something completely.*

He ignored everything on the inside that told him he was right, that it wouldn't make any difference, that cabins didn't equal children. That the ocean had only done to Alexis what she'd tried to do to herself so many times yet never managed. That death would always come when you couldn't prevent it, rolling you over and over until your skull, at last, met something harder. That when she'd left for India right out of the hospital, she had turned her back on everything he'd done to try and help her. What's India got for you anyway? What's there you can't find here? *Everything, Dad. And by God I mean that. Everything.*

—Alright. If it means that to you...

—Not for me – she refuted – Jesus. This is for you.

—For me.

—How can you not get that?

A loss like that. Equal.

The path to the shore was free of blow-down. It was just a tree-lined tunnel leading to the lake, crisp with moonlight. He spotted a dead cedar off the path and grabbed a hold of its trunk, tugging its grey burl of branches onto the trail. This would do it. He didn't agree he needed to lose something more. Alexis had been both of theirs. You don't make up for something broken by breaking something else, he reasoned. But this would prove it for her and that's what was needed to move on.

The tree barely fit through the door of the cabin. He bent his knees and pulled with force. A branch hooked under the drying rack and the two dinner plates smashed to the floor. Like the wake of a boat a trail of copper leaves followed him in. He could have started it on the porch but it would be a better fire this way, from the inside. A curl of birch bark held the flame alight as he brought it past the tent to the porch and then through the door. Was it true he was unbearable? That she'd resent him? Would they recover on the surface yet somewhere deep beneath, down the line, this would thunder into them again, collapsing roofs, sweeping away buildings, another child, igniting forgotten underground fires?

—Fuck you – he exhaled as he lit the tree. *Fuck you.*

The dry cedar caught fire with more speed than he expected. The branches hissed and twined as the hungry flames built. It was close enough that the easy chair soon caught and then the wooden cabinets, which brought the fire over to the wall. He'd never seen one spread so quickly. It poured over the surfaces like a liquid and then sat still to dig in its stubborn teeth. It licked at the hems of the curtains then shot up the walls toward the ceiling. It leapt the wooden stairs and then started in on the roof.

At first from outside he could barely tell it was on fire. Drizzles of smoke escaped from under the roof's overhang, more like a wet sock that steamed as it dried. Muffled pops, the faint sound of crackling, then the warm, earthen glow of someone curled up inside reading a book with a beer and old moccasins. In the loft window the flames took hold of the plaid curtain and mauled it down.

A loss like that. Sure.

He stood confronting the burning cabin in the dark of the damp grass and dialed the phone.

—Did you?

—Yeah. Just now.

—Thank God – she said – Thank you, oh thank God.

—I don't feel any better.

—You will – her voice sounded lighter, relieved – I promise you will.

He turned his back to the clearing and followed the path to the lake. The water seemed black and distant, as though it contained something sinister inside it that he would forever connect to what it had done to Alexis, as though its reflection mirrored back at him something more than just the shredded moon. The guilt of a good lie, perhaps – the kind people tell themselves with a straight face for a lifetime. Or the pale of her skin with all the sadness it had collected from some place he was never invited into. The red of her bandaged wrists and how in his mind he'd always held on to her, clinging even harder as she fought and struggled to get away. His girl. *Unbearable.*

Then, as if to wound it, he picked up a rock and threw it. The surface shattered, swallowing the hole in its splash. In endless, detached circles, the moonlight rippled outward and then gradually reformed. He could break its reflection a thousand times, with a thousand rocks, and always the moon would repair itself. Invariably the water's surface would heal. On the far edge of the lake, the beam from the lighthouse spun in slow rhythmic flashes. Down here he couldn't hear the fire, just the soft vacuum of forest and the constant rustle of waves onto shore stone.

Soft Coral, Sinking Pearl

Myaing renamed herself Mali the moment the lights of the patrol boat had extinguished behind the breakers. Hidden up the beach behind a fallen palm trunk, she listened as the surf buried the throb of the engine like shovels of wet sand. As far as she could tell, she'd been the only one to make it to shore. The soldiers must have hauled the others back into the boat under the frantic spotlight that illuminated the open-nosed machine guns that sprayed out their ammunition so endlessly. She studied the water for any sign of her sister: Nu was the stronger swimmer and might already be waiting farther up the beach. Mali's clothes and hair were drenched, her tiny chest heaving with exertion and adrenaline as she pressed herself down into the dark warmth of the foreign sand.

Thailand. *Thailand.*

She repeated the word over and over to herself, her hands gripping into the beach – a billion tiny fragments of this new country.

The larger boat had approached in total darkness about five hundred metres from the shore. Suddenly to their port side, there had been nearly a dozen soldiers shouting with weapons aimed. The Thai had been too quick and ferocious to understand, but everyone in her wooden rowboat knew how to translate *gun*. Half of them had leapt over the side when the light from the patrol craft switched on. The older ones crouched against the bottom ribs of the boat, ducking their heads beneath the seat planks as if the beam itself could wound them. Then the soldiers began to fire.

Myaing dove as deep as she could. Thrashing sounds sank down from the surface as others jumped in after her. Bullets whizzed mechanically through the water and shattered the coral in sharp but muted detonations. Reaching a depth where she had to depressurize her ears, she began swimming forward with the push of the waves. When her chest began to burn, she pulled herself up to the dark surface. From somewhere in the black, she heard Nu's voice scream out for her – *Myaing! Myaing!* – but she gulped another lungful of air and then plunged again. There was something about diving away from the sound of her sister's cries that made the nerves in her skin vibrate their cold, as if the water had deliberately wanted to come between them, to drive them apart like the wedge of teakwood their father had used to split bamboo. *Promise we won't wait for each other*, Nu had whispered, her thin arms tight around her sister's waist. *We'll meet up on shore. Just keep swimming. Promise me, Myaing.* She had to command her body to continue towards land; it hurt like a cramp in her heart.

Eventually, her outstretched hands contacted sand. She crawled from the surf up the beach and ran into the darkened jungle hoping the light from the full moon hadn't given her away. The sound of Nu's cries roared in her head against the insect noise: *Myaing!*

—Change your name immediately – her father had advised – And you must know, my precious goose, there will be no point mourning for us. The moment you feel Thailand beneath your feet, send us a prayer, change your name and forget Burma – Then he looked at Nu, furrowing his brow into creases that reminded her of freshly planted rows of rice. In the wet of his eyes, minnows reached their lips towards the surface, breaking it into ripples.

Past the breakers, the lights of the army boat crested with the waves and then vanished. She scanned the surf for any sign that Nu or anyone else from her boat had made it to shore. She waited motionless as bark in the lanky shadows of the coconut trees that bisected the sand down to the water. When a distant succession of gunshots cracked in Mali's ears, their shaggy caps didn't flinch; the moon didn't bother to blink.

▲ ▲ ▲

The wooden porch of the palm hut was littered with empty bottles and cigarette butts. Mali knocked on the door before entering. She set down her bucket of cleaning supplies in the corner of the room like a full vase of plastic flowers. She stripped the foam mattress of its sheets and pillowcases, tied the mosquito net in a knot and then set about tidying the hut. Except for gathering the garbage and sweeping the sand back out to the beach, the only job left was to empty the pail of used paper from beside the toilet. *Farang*, she had come to learn, were disgusting and they didn't know how to contain their own shit. *All a human needs to use is water* – Mali thought, emptying the putrid pail – *What about the process could be simpler? Why leave so much paper behind like a prize to be found?* Monkeys they were, at play with their own excrement.

The backpackers would sleep until the sun had already begun its downward curve, reflecting in the stale puddles of vomit pocking the sand outside their beach bars from the previous evening. Into the mornings, their music would thump through the woven siding of her hut and she'd lay awake under the blur of her mosquito net wondering how long it would take before she could begin to work in the kitchen with Luang and the rest of the Burmese women. She would listen to them chattering softly in her native language about the husbands and children they'd left behind in Yangon or Mandalay or the smaller villages along the coast that nobody in the world, besides them, even knew existed.

Every few weeks a new Burmese girl arrived on the beach looking for work. It was as though Phram could smell her foreign scent of desperation as she crawled from the sea. For now, it was Mali's turn to choose. If she did what he wanted, maybe then Phram would say – *Mali, from today you work in the kitchen* – as he led the newest sea-washed girl into his hut and latched the door.

What a price to pay – she thought – *cancelling out the last private part of yourself.* She wondered if it could possibly be worth it and what her sister and brother and father would say.

—Phram gets what he wants – Luang spat on the ground into the mango peels – He'll make you take it up your ass, that dirty pecker. I should poison his *khao soi*, but the trouble is he's too clever.

—He'll smell it.

—He has a nose like a tapir. Hand me that plate – Luang said – He's too ugly to get a girlfriend so he's bitter. But if you sleep with him, he'll move you in here. Think of that! You could cook with me in the kitchen.

—I don't mind cleaning.

—Phram says Burmese girls give the best head. Do you even know what that is?

—Yes – Mali lied – I know.

—Believe me, it isn't fair, but you make twice as much here in the kitchen. During high season, you won't even be thinking of Burma. And just think, if you met a handsome foreigner. Would you fall in love with someone carrying a cleaning bucket?

Mali peered over the counter to where the *farang* were. Hammocks criss-crossed the wooden deck, coils of mosquito repellant lit beneath the sagging crescents. They ashed joints in large beer bottles and wore black market T-shirts sewn in Bangkok. Phram was standing at one of the hammocks cooing in English with a red-haired *farang* girl. All Mali could see were knots of the girl's dreadlocks tangled like a lump of brain coral.

—I think they're horrible, Luang. Where could they possibly come from that they're so happy to turn their skin brown anyway?

Luang's knife slid through the yellow flesh of the mango, dissecting off cubes with the blade – Do you know Kulap from down the beach? Paradise Bungalows? She makes her own cream that whitens your skin in only one day. You'd need two days, Mali, because you're so black. But I'm sure she would give you a discount.

—I'm not so black.

—You're the darkest girl here. But don't worry. *Farang* like black skin – Luang's laugh looked like the chopped up mango. She hiked up her shorts made from pink cotton printed with penguins and then took the plate over to the counter.

—Phram! – she groaned – Take this to the boys at the pool table.

—Go fuck yourself – he said in Thai, not even looking over from the girl's hammock. His hands rested on the fabric sides like the gunwales of a boat – Can't you see I'm busy?

—Sure – she grumble to Mali – As busy as the asshole of a pig.

Luang slid out from behind the bar, crossed the deck and set the plate beside the three boys playing pool. They stood like awkward roosters, their bellies out and shirtless, scratching at the sweaty nooks beneath their swim shorts. Mali's brother Than was what she considered a handsome man, not these sun-rashed *farang* patched with tattoos.

—*Dis is Mary Kissmas mango* – Luang said, giving a light bow, her English deeply accented.

—You order that, Miles? – one of them said.

—No – the one named Miles said.

—Hey, Carl. You order a fucking Merry Kiss-my-ass mango?

—Yeah, I did. Screw off, why don't you.

—Think I can get her to feed it to me?

—Try it.

—Fuck off, Bosh. Leave her be.

—Yeah, well – he snapped up a piece with his fingers – you can take her. She's got a fat nose anyway.

—Hey. Can I get a beer? - the one named Miles said - A large one? Chang's alright.

—*One large Chang* – Luang said.

—Yeah. *Kap koon krup.*

—Clap poon crap - the one named Bosh laughed - What the hell, man. You speaking Thai now?

—Fuck off - Miles said, and then leaned over the pool table to take his shot - You're a jerk sometimes.

Mali didn't want to deal with *farang* directly like Luang had to. She had never seen so much white skin before coming to Ko Yao. Their bodies were shaped like octagons that turned crimson in the sun. Between cleaning each hut, she'd watch them slam themselves against the towering waves, their arms and legs emerging from the froth as they frolicked like albino horses. There was something hypnotic about watching them scan the horizon for the largest crests then turn towards the shore, paddling furiously until their bodies lifted atop the curling swells and then rode like planks nearly to the shore. For hours they played this game with the sea. To her envy, they had no fear of the water, no fear of the sun, of drugs. No fear of anything that might hurt them. Mali opened the door of the last empty hut, the gecko lizards darting across the beams of the porch.

As she stepped inside the hut, the smell hit her hard. She covered her nose with her arm, set the cleaning bucket down and moved cautiously around the room as though not to startle the culprit into releasing any more of its reek. At the far corner of the bed a crumpled-up top sheet lay near the window. Something about its colour, its position was already strange – like it had been rolled and placed there deliberately, as far away from the doorway as possible.

—*Farang...* - she said to herself - *How can the universe work this way?*

—Don't expect it to be fair - her brother Than had said, his chin freshly shaven, his black hair still dripping from his bath in the stream - Life will be harder for you. Women mean different things here. It's not fair, Myaing, but it's your turn. Then maybe in the next life it will be mine.

Mali imagined herself in a previous life as an oyster slowly churning out pearls. And then a mother whale drifting over the coral with a calf at her belly.

The sheet unrolled like a giant ball of orange grease. On the mattress, the vomit stain bloomed outward, an aureole of wetness surrounding a heavy nucleus of textured rust.

—Mali...there you are - a voice cooed at the doorway. It was Phram.

—I didn't know you were there. Look. What a mess those ones made in here.

—Show me. I don't see anything – Phram stepped inside and closed the door. She could see something dark and unfiltered in his eyes. Coffee grounds. Poison dirt. A raven's beak puncturing snake eggs.

—Look. Here – she said – What a mess.

—Where, Mali?

Coming from behind, Phram's palms covered her bony shoulders, gripped and then pushed her forward onto the bed. The wet of the mattress stain soaked through her hair against her face. That gag of foreign excrement, utter acid, the way Phram pinned her down with all his weight and fumbled with her shorts like he didn't know if he should take them off completely. Then with his hand on the back of her skull pushing her face farther into the mattress, the tip of his cock pressed up against her anus like Luang had warned.

Mali screamed into the sheets. She struggled a hand free, reached behind her and grabbed at the meat of his dick. She moved it down against her vagina and without pause he thrust its full length inside. If the body had a fault line, a place where it was prone to split in two, Phram had found it, then set about cleaving it open.

—...but you Burmese girls are so good at taking it up the ass – his lips panted at the crest of her ear – What makes you so special...You immigrant girls pretend you don't know how business works...You want to stay in the kitchen, huh?...How do you think the other bitches got to work there?

Outside on the beach, some *farang* boys were singing about Christmas. Their voices were sharp and off-key, more bellowing than song. She'd heard the holiday had something to do with trees in cold weather, coloured strings of lights and bells, an unwanted baby who claimed to be king. She remembered the missionaries in her small town of Myeik painting a cardboard baby and propping it in a plastic washtub outside the neighbourhood monastery. *Saviour of the world* – they'd called it triumphantly. Why the coming of this king was so exciting for these *farang*, she didn't know. Just a cardboard baby adrift in a bucket.

—...probably full of shit anyways – Phram shuddered as he withdrew – And you reek like a rotten durian. Clean up your pants then finish what you were doing. That was the worst fuck of my life.

Her breath had caught in her windpipe like a shell. She waited until Phram had left before trying to dislodge it. It was the shape of a sob coated in coral. She sat upright on the edge of the bed and bit into the flesh of her arm as the sound, minutes too late, forced its way up from her throat. The two halves of her body felt as though they would fly apart and open up a giant cavern filled with deadly gas. The hair on her vagina was slick with Phram's cum. Red, her fingertips touched the tack of her blood. She slowly peeled the hair from her cheek, pulled up her shorts and crossed the room, descended the stairs to the shore, then padded across the boiling sand into the turquoise sea fully clothed. When the warm wave came, she ducked beneath the surface, held her breath and listened to the clack of shells as the sea wore them down into grains of sand.

—I'll chop his dick off and feed it to his mother – Luang said, slamming her cleaver down, halving a papaya – That son of a bitch. What did I tell you?

—It was over soon enough – Mali said.

—That doesn't mean anything. What a monster. Did he even say he'd move you in here?

—No.

—You see? He wants to do you up the ass. That's what he likes but he's too embarrassed to put his hands on a boy. Come here. I'll make you *mohinga* like they sell at Sule Paya in Yangon.

Mali sat behind the counter watching the *farang* laze in their hammocks. Cigarette and ganja smoke spiraled upward from their thick fingers, veiling the images on the gigantic screen that kept them comatose for months on end. During the day, they sprawled in the sun like wilted squid. At night their skins turned dark as the peasants who worked the rice fields.

—Why do they come here? – Mali asked her – What do they do?

—For the parties. Didn't you know? Ko Yao is famous for them. Phram sells them cheap drugs and they dance on the beach until the morning.

—Like a festival?

—Yes. Like that. That's what the army boat is for.

Why would a festival need soldiers? she thought. Her world felt too small for so many *farang*. Myeik had been a quiet city of pearl farmers and shrimp fishermen, cut off even from the rest of Burma except for the long, bandit-ridden highway that ran through the jungle up the Malay Peninsula. After her brother left to teach at the University of Yangon, her world had shrunk to the dimensions of her family's hut. Nu would sweep the dirt yard clean each morning while Myaing tidied the space around the stove, her father cross-legged in the shade mending the nets the shrimp fishermen would use for harvesting. She thought of her sister. What had happened to her? Along with the hundreds of others who'd jumped over the sides of boats onto the beaches of Thailand, she feared she might never know.

Forget Burma. Her father's eyes were sacks of sadness buried in despondent sockets. He had paid for their passage to Thailand by selling three terraces of their family's rice field. He had stood at the door to their hut as she and her sister walked off to the dock to join the others at the boat. Something about leaving him in that yard with a half-bag of rice and a few sticks of noodles that would last him a week at most, about picturing him cooking at the fire alone, the loneliness of his eating, that one night in the future of their new lives when he would go to sleep and not wake up. It felt worse than torture to the sisters. Nu's sobs had soaked warm onto Myaing's shoulder, her tiny rib cage heaving as they walked towards the boat.

Luang and Mali lay beneath the mosquito netting listening to the thump of the music echo over from the party on the next beach. Checkering the net with segments, the full moon shone through the woven palm siding.

—Tonight is Christmas – Luang said – They'll be dancing until lunchtime tomorrow at least.

—Such horrible sounds to dance to.

Luang said – Here. Put your head on my chest. You can listen to the hole in my heart.

—Where? – Luang's breasts felt small as rambutans.

—Here – she took Mali's fingers – If you press down, you can feel it.

Mali felt nothing but the small arches of bone beneath Luang's skin.

—Does it hurt?

—What kind of a question is that? No one can ever feel it as well as I can. They don't even believe me when I tell them.

The thump of the music carried down through the jungle as though the trees didn't exist. She didn't know what a party like that could possibly look like, but she imagined huge circles of *farang* stomping wildly beneath canopies of Christmas lights, celebrating the fact they'd received their cardboard saviour while the rest of the world wandered in suffering searching for theirs. Mali prayed that somehow Nu had made it to shore and was on that beach, listening to the same hypnotic rhythms, thinking of Burma while trying to sleep.

—Tell Phram you want to work in the kitchen – Luang said – He owes you that much at least. And don't worry, the pain goes away. Anyways, it's not like you have a hole in your heart to be worried about. At least your twat will heal.

Against the horizon, the army boat floated like its own island, a gigantic continent of moonlit soldiers brought in to patrol the crowd for drugs and weapons. Boats from the next beach throbbed around the small promontory all night and into the morning, ferrying the partiers back to collapse on their sandy mattresses.

Mali woke after Luang had already left for the kitchen. The hut felt unusually quiet, like a forest of pillows had been pressed against all windows and joints, insulating the small room from the outside. She had just thrown her legs over the side of the bed when she heard Phram's voice outside, the glass rattling in the panes as he pounded on the door. A spiral drilled into Mali's stomach and spat up panic. He was drunk.

—Mali, you ugly bitch, let me in! – and then – You know as well as anyone what it takes to work in the kitchen.

—I'm busy. I'm getting dressed and then I have to clean...

Phram's head was a swaying charcoal shadow on the window curtain. He pressed in closer.

—Cunt! You'll do what I say...Luang says you wanted to work in the kitchen. The ugliest whores always want to stick together.

—I have to work, Phram. There is cleaning to do.

—Since when can Burmese even clean their own assholes – he banged harder – Open up!

—Phram! *Phram*! Get your frog-shaped ass away from there! – a voice shouted from farther away – Something's wrong with the ocean!

—...wrong with the ocean... – Phram slurred – I'll be back for you, foreigner...

Mali watched the shadow recede at the window, then heard Phram turn his feet and move to the edge of the porch. She peeled back the curtain. Phram's bare back stumbled away from the hut across the sand, all that venom in him sloshing to either side as he went. Then she peered out at the sea.

Like a skull that's just been scalped of its hair, the beach lay bone-smooth, barren of its water except for shallow divots leaping with fish. Knots of coral that had hidden beneath the water now spotted the distance.

—The sky pulled the sea back! - a little Thai girl screamed, her arms and legs a starfish as she ran out onto the expanse. Long-tail boats wilted on their sides where their anchors had kept them. Gatherings of foreigners stood with their cameras, posed on the sand or sprinting around to nowhere, the way people do in freshly opened spaces. Mothers took the hands of their children and walked them out, babies in arms - a curiosity best experienced as a family.

Mali opened the door and caught the tang of mineral earth in the air. Luang was standing at the bottom of the stairs with two plastic buckets.

—Come on! - she shouted - We'll collect the shellfish! There's a million of them stuck to the rocks.

—Is Phram out there?

—Phram can suck my dick - she said - We won't share any of them with him anyway. Roasted with some papaya, they'll be delicious! Come on, Mali! He'll never try anything with so many people around. Bring your knife so you can pry the shells loose.

Mali tied her hair behind her head and followed Luang down onto the beach. The boys from the pool table had thrown off their shirts and were racing towards the horizon. Like hooves, their feet sprayed clumps of sand up in the air behind them. The girl with the red dreadlocks had walked out as far as she could on the new sand.

—What do you think happened? – Mali asked.

—Who even knows. Let's go over to those rocks. Look at all the Thais with their buckets. How poor we all look scrounging for our dinner. And the *farang* certainly laughing at us. I don't even care though.

It felt strange to be so far from the huts yet still on land. They seemed perched on the edge of a desert cliff, having leapt clear of some catastrophe. Even stranger was the quiet of the beach, the water having pulled out so far they could no longer hear the waves. The broken seashells were coarser out here before they would eventually grind their way into the fine white powder of the shore. The new surface was cold and almost slippery beneath her feet – a muck of algae like damp fur. She wondered if she would find old bullets lodged in the reef where soldiers had shot down into the water at other Burmese girls jumping from boats or if the coral had lactated its bone around them until they disappeared entirely into distresses of scar. She wondered what it would feel like to be buried by something slow as pearl; the millennia of deposits it would take as the waves continued overhead. What she could protect herself from if only she had the ability to surround herself in bone.

Mali found a clump of mollusks a little ways from where Luang had crouched down and started picking. At the base of the rocks, tiny yellow and sapphire fish darted around in sparkling pools. A few already pulsed on the sand, exhausted.

—Are you getting many? – Luang shouted – They're coming off so easily!

—I'm getting some – Mali shouted back – Yes, I'm getting lots now.

Mali looked over in Luang's direction and then spotted Phram farther out, throwing hunks of sand at the boys from the pool table and then lighting a cigarette. Her insides scalded as she watched him. The boys chased each other in circles like street dogs with no boundaries or curbs to contain them.

—It will never seem fair – her father had said, rubbing his thumb along the lacquer coating the silky inner curve of a clam shell – But life doesn't promise us fair. As soon as we realize that, the happier we will be with what's given to us. We Burmese have learned to be happy with things as they are.

She looked down at the sand and then, like rain on a puddle, the minnows broke the surface of her eyes. *Things as they are.* Things as they are were painful and frantic as choking, it didn't matter how many clams she collected for dinner. She missed Nu. She missed Burma, her father, the smell of their fire in the hut, the way the brutality of the army had pulled everyone closer together despite trying to pry it apart.

When she thought about Than, her tears tumbled over her cheeks and dropped into the pools of blue fish. How proud she had been of her brother. No one else in her family had even been to school, let alone become a professor. She used to rub his feet while he read aloud from his textbooks, so many words she didn't know. Just the shape of them in Than's mouth was enough to make her proud.

—I'm going in – she shouted to Luang, who had moved to a new rock – Maybe I ate something funny. I don't feel well...

—Fine, I'll stay out here and collect them all. But leave me your pail. I'll fill it too.

Mali dropped her bucket and began across the large stretch of sand towards the restaurant huts.

Once, when walking home from the market, Myaing had grabbed Than's arm and held him close.

—Don't do that – Than grinned – Everyone will think we're a couple.

—I don't mind – she said – It's to show how proud of you I am.

He nodded his smooth handsome face towards a soldier.

—Would you be proud of me if I joined the army?

—Don't be silly, brother. The army doesn't want soldiers who speak English.

—Who told you I speak English, anyway?

—Nu did. She heard you practicing.

—That parrot! I'll teach her to squawk like one.

—I am proud. And besides, professors in Yangon speak a dozen languages, don't they?

—I suppose – Than said – Some of them. But you too, Myaing, will have to learn English when you leave for Thailand.

—Then we can speak together in secret and no one will understand what we are saying.

Myaing's favorite part was that he didn't pull his arm away. They walked like a blissful couple until their father's hut.

Nearly to the shore, Mali saw groups of *farang* begin to stand and gaze out at the horizon behind her. *Phram is probably harassing some little girl*, she thought. *Maybe even Luang.* She didn't care. She wished the water hadn't gone so she could inhale full lungs of air and drop to the bottom where he could never find her.

When the *farang* on the shore began to yell, Mali finally turned. The horizon was a dark band of blue that lacerated the sky and ocean. It seemed perpetually stuck at a distance, yet something kinetic stirred inside it – incremental shifts so subtle her eye couldn't catch them directly, the way stars only sparkled when you looked between them at the black.

—What is that? – the *farang* were shouting – What's going on?

—Maybe an earthquake affected the water?

—Look, all the Thais are coming in.

—What is it?

—It's heading towards the beach!

—Jesus Christ. Maybe we should warn them?

The huge bow of the army boat suddenly leapt vertically. A cry of disbelief crescendoed from the shore as the whole enormous vessel was thrown backwards and then twisted sideways, completely capsizing under the giant roils of water. Phram and the boys stood making odd, frantic gestures at the wave, provoking it closer, their high-pitched laughter fully audible over the growing roar. But then they could see the speed of it – the details of the foam, the ribbon of blue that had turned into a thick band of grey that threw up flares of spray as it churned over itself into the shallower water, galloping towards the beach. Something tight rose inside Mali's chest, something in the shape of fear but that felt more like a lung starved of its pull for oxygen. Against Phram's height, the wave rose five or six times higher, taller than the biggest buildings in Myeik, taller than even the palm trees, it seemed. She saw Luang turn and grab both buckets, running as fast as she could with their awkward weights. *Mali! Mali!* Her toes suddenly caught the rise of a divot and her face scrunched as it impacted the ground, the spilled clams an instant constellation on the sand.

—Don't worry, you goose. I'm just going to hold your head under – Nu said, standing up to her breasts in the crystal cold stream that ran through the teak forest behind their family's rice field – It doesn't hurt. You just inhale deeply, close your eyes, then go under.

—I'll need to breathe, sister. That's my biggest fear. I'll panic.

—That's why I'll hold you under. It's better if I do.

—It's only an excuse for you to kill me, I bet. Than will beat you if you hurt me.

—I taught Than to hold his breath the same way. Ask him if you like. Anyways, after a minute, once you're used to it, I'll come down there and stay with you. We'll hold our heads under together.

The teak forest ruffled sprays of the dry season sun through its leaves and they landed like canaries on Nu's wet hair and shoulders. Myaing felt the current shoving across her inner thighs, that perpetual force that pressed her skin like a fist and then furled backwards on itself in a chorus of ripples.

—Hold your breath, sister. Ready?

The water hit her face. Then she was under.

Like algae, the stream pulled her hair in its direction. Something clacked or ticked loudly in her ears and Myaing realized it was the water lifting and dropping the pebbles against each other, tumbling them towards the ocean. For a moment, it sounded like music, like the hooves of water buffalo striking stone, her father splitting stalks of bamboo. But the sensation of not breathing – of not having the choice to breathe – shot pellets of panic up her throat. The unfairness of it all, of being completely immersed in it, at its mercy, overwhelmed Myaing as Nu's palms covered her skull and kept her from being able to surface. *I'll come down there and stay with you, sister. I'll hold you under and then come stay with you after.* But when, Nu? When? That minute felt so impossibly long. Long and cruel and painful and solitary. Then Nu's grip suddenly loosened and she felt her sister's hands move down to her shoulders, the soft brush of her black hair flowing towards her, both of them like adjacent pearls clutching each other, sinking to the bottom of the stream.

Jesus Very Thin and Hungry

—I can understand a fear of flying – Cassie said finally – We *should* be afraid of heights. The sky never pretended to be hospitable to us. It's incredible we're even alive on the ground.

—Less so than the ocean? – Miles drained the can of tuna into the sink and unscrewed the lid from the jar of mayonnaise.

—What can you do if the ocean scares you? You can't even take a boat or go parasailing. What about swimming? Are you just going to pace along the beach?

—Nobody travels by boat anymore – Miles said – Life would be so much worse with a fear of flying. You can bypass the ocean completely in a plane. Besides, there's nothing relaxing about the sea. Nothing could be more unpredictable.

Whenever Miles made the tuna salad, Cassie always felt he added too much mayonnaise. That oblivious, wasteful excess was another one of those annoyances that so often felt amplified because of the presence of so many others.

—I just don't enjoy the taste of fish – he defended – And I think we should respect each other's fears.

Cassie assured Miles she was going to buy that bikini anyway and that he could lay on a lounge chair and watch her swim if he wanted. Wryly, her voice had intoned *for all I care*. It had been five years since they had attempted to backpack around India, after which Cassie decided she wasn't the roughing-it type and would fare better at an all-inclusive. During their travels, she had gradually revealed to Miles her disgust at the hostels' bed linens, still bearing odious traces of the previous occupants. She cringed at the residue on the Indian Rail seats that turned slippery with the heat and movement. For Cassie, a walk around the streets of Calcutta was tantamount to a backstage pass into a circus of horrors. No matter how much goodness and light Miles claimed emanated from a beggar's eyes, Cassie believed the perfect vacation consisted of rows of lounge chairs lined up like dominoes, mounted by leggy bodies basted with coconut oil and truncated by flapping beach umbrellas.

—Why can't we travel somewhere inland, like Mongolia or Paraguay? – Miles asked – Besides, the ocean gives some countries an unfair advantage. I'd feel better supporting one without a coastline.

Cassie didn't respond but switched on their small kitchen television. A man was being interviewed on the news. A long unkempt beard fizzled down to his chest and nickel-sized blisters like popped bubble wrap annexed most of his skin. The rest of his body was wrapped in a bright orange rescue blanket. In a thick Spanish accent, the reporter described that after two hundred and sixty-nine days the two Mexican fishermen had been found alive off the coast of Taiwan and appeared "very thin and hungry but otherwise healthy." The man who had been rescued was named Jesus Vidaña.

—After nine months lost at sea, thin and hungry doesn't seem like a terrible diagnosis – Miles said, transfixed. The sight of another survivor, someone who had ridden the cusp of catastrophe and then, like a champion surfer, emerged out the other side, was enough to make Miles feel less alone. If there was Jesus, there were also others who could sympathize with how it felt to suddenly arrive back on dry land, so much having changed in the meanwhile.

—They must have been starving – Cassie said – Unless they ate each other. Now there's something I'm petrified of. That's my fear. Hunger will lead a person to do anything.

—Raw turtles and sea birds – Miles corrected absently – That's how they survived.

Cassie thanked God for their Taiwanese neighbours, Sun and Chen, the kind of predictable people who hung their laundry on the clothesline year round, who travelled to sensible places like Miami or Rome. They highly recommended Mexico. There were plenty of beaches so she could feel like she was on vacation, but there were still temple ruins and that smell of burning trash Miles needed to feel like he was really travelling.

—Make sure the hotel has a swimming pool – Miles called – I won't be going near the ocean.

The pennants of white briefs and light purple panties provided Cassie with an inexplicable but neutralizing comfort she knew Miles wouldn't understand. She imagined their neighbours' garments spelled out some sort of code – a love poem from Sun to Chen as cryptic and beautiful as the cage-like glyphs of their kanji. From the kitchen sink, she watched their laundry flap in the August breeze like maritime semaphore while, in the corner of their yard, their dog Piglet tugged holes in a black garbage bag. Cassie heard Chen's voice scold Piglet in broken English as the dog's greasy snout emerged clasping an old chicken carcass studded with Q-tips.

Sun and Chen were small-boned and friendly and could be trusted to water Cassie's collection of houseplants. Anyone who still used a laundry line could automatically be trusted in Cassie's books. Trust wasn't something you could earn but was something demonstrated in every one of your actions. Despite everything else, Cassie knew she could trust Miles implicitly: Anyone who clung to a palm tree for six hours deserved it.

From behind the refrigerator door, Miles mumbled to Cassie that it didn't matter where in the world you went, some-one was bound to be starving to death. His comment sum-moned inside her the anxious feeling that she might run into one of them casually, maybe even walking home from work one evening. Starving people could be lurking anywhere. There was something true and credible inside that possibility and it terrified her.

—I'd have given up hope – Miles said.

—You couldn't pay me to eat raw birds – said Cassie, silently translating the drying underwear.

▲ ▲ ▲

The receptionist had greeted them cordially as they checked into the four-star all-inclusive fronting a beach of perfectly groomed sand and rolling aqua surf.

—You have arrived at the right time – she smiled nervously – I'm honoured to inform you that Jesus himself will be a guest at our resort during your stay.

The woman's accent pronounced it *Hay-zoos.*

—That's right – she repeated – Jesus.

—I don't know who that is – Cassie said, eager to scour the complimentary minibar – Someone famous?

—Jesus is a source of pride for all Mexicans, señora – the receptionist informed them – Jesus Vidaña, a truly remarkable human being whose trials and tribulations have inspired all Mexicans to a deeper faith in El Señor. Here is the key to your suite.

That afternoon Miles spotted Jesus by the swimming pool. In a loose blue Speedo and plastic gift-shop sunglasses, he reclined beneath a metal palm tree that cast a stylized frond of shade over his skin tanned the colour of perfect toast. Every twenty minutes or so, between flipping the pages of his cracked paperback, he would coat his torso with a veneer of oil he kept beside his lounge. Miles chewed his cocktail straw into a kinked wad of plastic. He watched Jesus reach his arms around to oil the backs of his shoulders. Faint marks where the blisters had healed spotted his lower back.

Miles stood and stretched casually, glancing out at the sea. Cassie was still floating on the neon green blow-up bed out where the water turned from turquoise to deeper blue. As he walked, the textured concrete semi-circles scraped into the pool deck annoyed the bottoms of his feet. In the air, a flock of gulls worried the sky in a matrix of winged arithmetic that dove in a swarm at loose french fries and empty Styrofoam containers.

Jesus' back was a slab of lean muscle that tapered down to an athletic waist. Black hair formed a V as it converged at his waistband and then disappeared between his buttocks. Miles had never approached a celebrity, not even a minor one. The thought caused a hollow yet bloated feeling to descend down into him like a hunk of chewing gum. More than anything though, Miles needed to speak with someone who could understand what he'd been through, a person who understood survival. If that man were really the Jesus from the news, he felt he should push all pride aside.

—Can I offer you help with that? - Miles asked softly as he approached. He felt awkward and blushed immediately. He sounded rehearsed, in a pornographic way.

Jesus Vidaña turned and lifted his sunglasses, studying Miles - *Si. Gracias.*

He was clean-shaven and his jet-black hair was trimmed short and brushed back off his forehead, but up close Miles felt that jolt of recognition. It was a different version of the Jesus he'd seen on television, but it was most certainly him.

The bottle was slick and Miles had to adjust his grip to press down adequately on the pump top. He squirted more oil than was necessary and worked it across the broad acreage of Jesus' golden back. Miles felt the texture of the healed blisters like Braille. A bead of oil descended through the lower patch of back hair like a hedge maze and disappeared down into Jesus' crack.

—*Could I ask you to do my legs also?* – He spoke with a Spanish accent that made Miles think of cedar planks and chin-up bars, bleach and tile setting on concrete.

—Of course – Miles offered. One must make oneself of as much service as one could to a man whose disaster outmatched one's own, he thought.

As Jesus rolled onto his stomach, fully extended, Miles looked out to the ocean, to the swimmers who frolicked and bobbed so heedless of the ocean's danger. Cassie had also rolled onto her front and was maneuvering the green blow-up bed in line with the incoming waves. Her head was turned to gauge the timing of the breaker and as it crested, she paddled furiously, skidding down the front of the curl and riding nearly to the shore. The look of joy on her face reminded Miles of a Down syndrome child who had just learned how to make hot dogs out of playdough.

—This might sound strange… – Miles' heart thumped in his chest – But have you ever been lost at sea?

Jesus turned to the side – *I could interpret that question in many ways. But yes, how did you know?*

—I don't know. I just remember you – Miles said, relieved – from the news… You ate seagulls for nine months. Fishermen rescued you.

—*That is some of what happened. The part that interests people…*

Miles hesitated, his hands pausing on Jesus' solid, warm hamstrings – Can I ask you a personal question?

—*Claro.*

—How do you still face the ocean? I mean, doesn't it scare you to be near it?

Jesus rolled over and lifted his sunglasses to rest on his forehead. Deeply set within thick lashes and brown eyes, his dark pupils were large and held fast to Miles' gaze. On their black canvases, Miles watched a small wooden boat lift and drop on the swells of an endless sea. Huddled together against the storm, the silhouettes of three men picked apart a gull, a blizzard of loose feathers catching the howling, disinterested wind.

—*It wasn't the ocean that scared me, señor. The ocean saved my life.*

▲ ▲ ▲

—What about Jerusalem? – Cassie had asked Miles as he rinsed the empty tuna can in the sink. She sat at the dinette, flipping through the newest edition of a library-rented *Israel* guidebook – It's far enough inland, isn't it? God, I don't remember anything from the Bible.

—Funny – Miles said – I don't think I remember anything either. I feel I should, but I don't.

—It's hard to hold on to what no longer inspires you – Cassie offered casually. After a pause, she declared – The feeding of the five thousand. That's a decent one. Something about all those hungry people suddenly having food. Happy multitudes with full stomachs. It's hopeful, isn't it?

—Jonah – Miles said, after some thought – That's mine, I guess. Minus the whole giant fish bullshit.

—Do you think if you were ever hungry enough you'd eat another person? – Outside, Sun was pegging a sentence of panties to the line. Cassie wondered if the message spelled *I can't anymore* or *You don't deserve me* – I'd really have to be starving – she continued absently – I don't enjoy hungry people.

—You're afraid they might do anything. That's why you dislike them.

—That's why I hated India. Do you remember I wanted to come home? Thank God I didn't go to Thailand with you, that's all I can say. Do you see how everything happens for a reason?

In India, Cassie had locked herself in the guesthouse for days on end. She hadn't wanted to go outside ever since they'd seen a body, thin as a skeleton but still alive, lying in a puddle of its own urine outside the Meenakshi temple. Like stale oatmeal plagued with raisins, blackflies had settled along its naked spine. A few metres down the street, a man stood with his arms crossed, leaning against the prow of his rickshaw, bored. Beneath its wheel, a small bird hopped in the dirt searching for crumbs among a crushed marigold garland. The man's chin tilted to his chest as he rubbed his eyes with his palms and yawned. The bird cocked its head and then swooped up to a branch that extended over the stone wall of the temple. From somewhere deep inside, a bell began to ring as if needing to break the scorching air for weighing too much. In the dust, a parade of ants scurried towards the liquid pooling around the body. Blocked, they stopped short and then detoured up the person's leg bone, crossing to its other side. Cassie had gasped when the skeleton suddenly shifted and the puddle began to expand across the dust before dripping down the curb into the gutter. She'd been petrified the creature would crawl towards her, crack her open with its cries for food, cling to her forever. From then on she'd wanted to leave India. In Hampi she'd been petrified of thieves. She hadn't been able to eat solid food since Agra. Worse was Varanasi where bodies were burned into charcoal mummies on top of the funeral pyres, billows of sparks shooting skyward from the hulls of their collapsing ribcages.

—Do you think it's possible to fear a place in theory? - Cassie asked.

Miles responded that most of what we fear is already theoretical and Cassie stared for a moment at the water swirling down the drain in a murky whirlpool and then out at the laundry line: *I can't anymore.* She wondered if it was possible to love something only in theory also.

▲ ▲ ▲

—It's just that I survived a disaster of my own - Miles said. He wiped the excess oil on his shins and sat straddling the lounge chair, facing Jesus. Since arriving, his own skin had taken on an effervescent caramel glow that made him feel like a glazed duck in a Chinatown window – I held onto a palm tree. It doesn't seem like much, but there were several waves.

—*For how long?*

—Six hours, thereabout. You ate seagulls. I know it doesn't compare.

—*It does* – Jesus said – *We both did what was necessary to survive.*

Jesus went on to explain to Miles how they'd been able to catch fish by making hooks with string from their clothing and wire picked from the engine. They dove into the water with ropes tied to their waist and harpooned sea turtles with a shard of metal lashed to an oar. He'd strangled the creatures with his hands as their flippers spasmed against the boat's wooden siding, their liquidy eyes blinking, weeping in slow motion. He described how he'd never expected how much would be packed inside that shell or how soft what keeps us alive is. After three months, he'd forgotten what trees looked like, how it felt to stand still. They'd collected rainwater in gasoline containers and stayed awake in shifts to scan the horizon for distant flashes of cargo ships or fishing vessels. One of the men had refused to eat the raw meat and starved to death. They'd lived with the corpse on board for two days before rolling it over the side. Finally, off the coast of the Marshall Islands, he and his friend had been rescued, two hundred and seventy days later, by a Taiwanese tuna trawler named *Koo's 102*. Miles stared at Jesus' hands as he talked, wondering if they looked any different as they strangled a turtle.

—Is there a girlfriend?

—Mine?

—No one comes to a beach resort alone. Am I wrong?

—You did – Miles said. Cassie had dragged the inflatable bed onto shore and she stood in the shallows, bending down every so often and picking at something beneath the waves that lapped at her ankles. Gulls circled above her, landed, then padded across the sand to the blow-up bed, pecking the sand around it.

—There's a girlfriend. She's enjoys resorts – Miles continued – She hated India. I forgave her for that though...

—She's beautiful when she's smiling – Jesus spotted Cassie – *She seems to enjoy the ocean.*

— ... I slept with a woman in Thailand – Miles responded, almost automatically – Before the tsunami, after Cassie went home.

The memory surfaced from a place Miles had buried deep beneath the events of the disaster, like a diver being pulled to the surface by a balloon of air. When the tsunami was over, he'd just been happy to be alive. The water had come for him and he'd survived. He'd been given a clear second chance and he'd squandered it immediately, insanely – More of a girl really... I didn't know at the time.

—A girl – Jesus said.

Miles watched Cassie lift the bottom of her foot and examine it. She cradled the blow-up bed beneath her arm and limped up the beach towards the pool, the toes of her foot curled as talons as she walked.

—I've never told her – Miles confessed – She admires me so much for making it through a disaster. How does someone not become what they survived?

—*It's much too late for that, señor* – Jesus answered calmly – *A disaster is exactly that, because of what it takes from you. Once it's happened, it's mandatory you lack a feeling of wholeness afterward. And don't expect to forget it. Like I said, it wasn't the ocean that scared me. Your girlfriend is coming this way. But I think it would be good for us to talk again. My heart tells me you need someone who understands catastrophe.*

Cassie stood on the far side of the pool by their empty lounge chairs squeezing the water from her ponytail. She squinted against the brightness, scanning for Miles in the pool and then on the chairs around the deck. For a moment, Miles hoped she wouldn't see him. He lowered his gaze at the deck, as he watched the water darken the concrete where the drops of sweat had gathered since he'd arrived at Jesus' chair. The tan line from his flip-flops made a deep Y shape on the top of his foot. To the right, a similar puddle had grown around Jesus' toes, small and almost feminine, but with wisps of black hair growing from the tops of each.

—Catastrophe... – Miles repeated.

—*Your girlfriend* – Jesus lowered his sunglasses – *She really has an exceptional body.*

Miles watched the puddle around his foot expand across the desert of textured surface until finally it made one single pool with the water around Jesus' feet. Miles suddenly felt better, as though the empty feeling had drained from him leaving him full and strangely satisfied – Yes, she does.

—Miles? – Cassie said from behind him.

He looked up at her shape silhouetted against the sun and blue sky. For some reason he thought of boat travel and jet skis and seashells being pulverized into perfect white sand.

—I cut my foot – Cassie said – Look.

She held it out, giving Jesus a cursory glance – I must have stepped on some glass... – The bottom of her sole was indented with the texture of the decking; sand had dried into the horseshoe crevices of her toenails.

—*Maybe it was a piece of shell?* – Jesus offered.

—No – Cassie looked at Jesus coldly – It was glass. I'm going inside to find a bandage. I'm starving too. I feel like I haven't eaten for days.

—It was nice to meet you – Miles said, standing – Congratulations on surviving your disaster.

—*The pleasure was mine. It gets better, as they say.*

—What did that mean? – Cassie asked, as they stepped into the air-conditioned lobby. After the pool decking, the burgundy carpet felt noticeably softer, more organic, like moss or the trimmed grass of a putting green. Years ago they must have permitted smoking inside; there was a faint odour of tobacco mixed with carpet shampoo.

—What did what mean?

—Congratulations on surviving your disaster. Who was that guy? And a Speedo? Really?

—He's Mexican.

—I don't think that's any excuse. God, I could eat a horse.

Cassie found a resort worker in a trim black uniform and showed him her injured foot. The man brought her arm around his neck and led her into a hidden corridor of supply and personnel offices. From inside the lobby, Miles watched Jesus run his fingers beneath the elastic of his bathing suit, smoothing the hair around his navel with the oil. He stood and looked out at the ocean, then lifted his foot to examine something on its sole. Behind him, a gull began to devour an empty Styrofoam plate, a ravenous clump of feathers. Hunger would lead a person to do anything, Miles thought. You could never know what horrible things you were capable of until you'd done them and then there was no taking them back. How many fish would it take to feed all five thousand? Miles wondered as he stood watching Jesus. How many humans to satisfy one giant fish?

The Road to Jerusalem
Goes Through Karbala

—A female bomber pretending to be pregnant detonated the first one... – Harim struggles to keep up with the pace of translation. He picks out bits the crowd of men shout at him – *...A male bomber also blew himself up as the ambulances arrived...*

Clusters of deflated balloons hang from a tower of amplifiers, motionless in the boiling afternoon. Black char sprays up an adjoining cinderblock wall, its dark umbra fanning outward as though painted on with a blowtorch – some arsonist's quick graffiti. Shredded, the remains of party streamers, once the same crisp white as the bride's dress, have long since been trampled. Concrete rubble and chunks of broken stone lay scattered across the scorched ground nearly to the road. Plastic chairs coated with skins of dust lay strewn around the car-sized crater. Where three men crouch staring into it, the hole gets deeper and the water turns from black to red. Behind them, the burnt-out wedding car, scorched and skeletal, a bouquet of plastic flowers melted off the rear bumper. A sudden breeze that smells like cardamom drafts a balloon out from under a chair and settles it behind the rim of the car.

An old woman draped in black appears in the doorway of the adjacent building. She wails in Arabic and carries a gold-framed portrait of the young bride. Her burka skims the pools of blood at her feet before she collapses, disconsolate, into the arms of her nephew or son or stranger. The crowd begins to push towards us, incensed into a suffocating nearness like an agitated herd preparing to stampede. As they push in around me, I lift the camera again to my eye and snap at their lamenting faces. This is for my protection. People will give a camera distance; they will give a woman with a camera all the distance she needs.

One man grabs my wrist and pulls me towards the edge of the crater. He points down into the water. Hovering just beneath the surface, the bride's slender hand with painted fingernails severed at the wrist. I aim through the viewfinder, pivoting my lens so the reflection of the man's grief-stricken face is reflected in the hand's open palm: a harrowing portrait framed in the crosshairs.

I release the shutter. Gorgeous.

Paul and I are at the opening of a Magnum exhibition of combat photography at the Art Gallery of Ontario in downtown Toronto. The whole CBC set crew is invited, though it was I, not Paul, who'd made arrangements for us to attend. Shot in Vietnam, Biafra, Afghanistan and Nicaragua, the images are a curated conglomeration of catastrophe, neatly framed, matted and aligned on the imperfect red brick walls. If you squint and stand at a distance, they take on the appearance of textured abstract prints, like neutral pastels crushed on concrete. It's a trick I play when I shoot so I can frame the geometry right, though Paul had once confessed that shapes and body parts weren't at all similar. For a camera technician, he's oddly oblivious to the basic principles of photography.

Standing in a towel at the bathroom sink after I'd blow-dried my hair, I told Paul that combat journalists like myself brought their respect to an exhibition like this one. With his crew from CBC, an open bar would seem like some fraternity challenge meant to be surmounted.

—Why do pictures require good behavior? - Paul combed his moustache - We're not at work, Les. For Chrissakes, loosen up.

—I'm only asking you to take it easy. I know the people there.

Know was intoned in a way that meant *don't embarrass me*, but Paul is as defiant as he is skilled at telling jokes. With a rocks glass in his hand, he stands in the corner of the gallery, his fellow camera technicians cracking up around him at regular intervals in loud rifts of laughter. Behind him and to his left is a large colour photograph of a group of Palestinian refugees freshly executed on the streets of Beirut. To his right, in black and white, a mother and her four children huddle by the bank of a muddy river in South Vietnam as overhead a gunman in a chopper lines them up.

—What's the definition of confusion? - Paul baits the group that begins to gather with each passing volley. The grin on his face tells me he's feeling pretty damn good about himself – Blind lesbians in a fish market.

The crowd of men is an eruption of molars and clanking glasses under arches of high-fives. His timing is impeccable, which makes it easier to despise him because he's so damned good at being lewd.

—Really, Les? – My best friend Greta feigns disgust and pulls me away.

—I asked him to behave – I apologize – You can't expect me to control a grown man.

But her eyes stay glued to him in that way I've seen a dozen women lock their gaze. The way I did when I was an enthusiastic intern studying him from the news desk as he adjusted the giant TV cameras.

Our reporting headquarters are stationed in the reception room of the old Emperor Hotel. Across the street, the Tigris meanders down the centre of Baghdad, a cool ribbon spanned by wide stone bridges that absorb the heat of the encroaching desert and then release it outward in ripples of shimmering air.

—...*The female bomber blew herself up as people were dancing and clapping, while the passing wedding party played music...* – Harim is on the telephone, switching between English and Arabic, with a local tip-off about a suicide attack in Karbala, a city seventy miles to the southwest – ...*the male bomber attacked soon after as police and ambulances arrived at the scene.*

—Deaths? – I ask.

—At least thirty-five...sixty-five wounded, including the bride and groom.

Harim is one of three Iraqi translators the CBC hired for the duration of the war to assist us in covering our stories. He's the only one of them who misses the irony that for him, war is a benefit. Or maybe he's the only one who just hasn't admitted it. He's solid as a tree with thick muscular forearms and a broad black moustache that offsets almost feminine eyes rimmed by enviable lashes. Even on days over forty degrees, he's still in long sleeves and pants, not a sheen of sweat grazing his forehead. Although it's a gross comparison, he's always appeared to me like a well-groomed, tidy Saddam.

—Why a woman, do you think? – I ask Carter, my assignment manager.

—Explosives are easier to conceal under a woman's clothing – Carter says – You aren't treated with the same suspicion as men.

—We should be – I say – We're lethal and devious and stop at nothing to get what we want. You've worked with me before, you should know that. I'm deranged.

—You're a sniper, Les. It's why we love you. I need you to go to Karbala today and scan your images to Toronto by this evening. Take Harim. He's got the best sense and knows the area.

I used to think photography was as close to the truth as one could get. It seemed impossible to lie to a camera, even more so when an arm's been blown off and its blood transforms into this perfect refractor of light that ultimately, in cruel and almost unjustifiable ways, renders the photograph a beautiful one. It's a tough paradox to swallow: beautiful blood. But atrocity releases some sort of lunatic aesthetic impulse inside me. It's why so many combat photographers are certifiable because we're confused by our attraction to death. Greta once told me I'd make the worst beauty pageant judge – my criteria are so skewed I'd get the winner entirely wrong.

An hour outside Baghdad, I ask Harim to pull over somewhere I can use the toilet. He turns into an oil truck weigh-station just off the highway on a patch of cleared desert. From behind a dusty pyramid of oranges at her market stand, a woman with deeply etched lines in her face directs me around the back.

When I open the wooden door to the toilet a hunched figure at the window turns: A black trapezoid catches the edges of the dim light source, rustling under the fabric of her burka. The air is thick as an attic's, that musk of nomadic women edged with spice caravan, algae and animal hide. At first, when she brings out her fingertips covered with blood I think she's been shot. A scrap of old fabric crumpled on the windowsill is mottled with red. From beneath her burka I am being scanned, analyzed and ignored.

The four toilets are shallow ruts fenced off by knee-high wooden doors. As I step into the stall, drop my pants and squat over the hole, I watch her continue to clean herself and wonder how they managed to cope with everything I would find so difficult. They hauled massive piles of wood strapped to their

backs and sweated it out on foot mile after mile inside those
body bags. Pregnant, they curled up in some deserted hut and
pushed out their baby in silence like a bitch delivering pups
beneath a table. They seem of stronger stock than their men
who keep them like mules for their endurance.

—Two condoms walk past a gay bar – Paul rallies again –
One says to the other, "Hey, fancy dropping in there and getting shit-faced?"

—Obscene – I hear Greta mumble. She stands a few feet
away studying a photograph of a mass grave, an incompre-
hensible tetris of joints and limbs askew, piled like discarded
chicken bones – I don't know how people get away with it.

—What do you call a gay man's scrotum?

—Jesus, Paul...

—Mud flaps.

—Les, is this even real? – Greta's face searches for some
sinew of explanation.

I wad a folded napkin from my bag and dab my crotch.
The trapezoid is at the rusted rain barrel rinsing her hands
when I exit the stall. Water sloshes from her palm and splashes
dust onto the hem of her burka and the mint green wall where
a colony of spiders have abandoned their webs. Shafting down
onto the crumbling paint, the light is a frenzy of molecules,
each one a rebel. Through the grid in the woman's eye screen,
I just barely catch a fractal of skin: cheek, eyebrow, lip. Some
creature is alive beneath that portcullis, some stalwart in-
habitant of either a prison or a citadel. She turns and drifts
across the floor, disappearing. From the woman outside, I buy

four oranges and two bottles of water. She uses one hand to place them into a bag, her other a stump truncated at the elbow.

—Nothing is how it should be – I think.

The truck's form shimmers through the heat of the scorched gravel as though from inside a furnace. Inside, the cab is air-conditioned. Harim lifts my camera bag off the seat, placing it between us as I get in. He shifts into drive and pulls back onto the road.

I say – I thought a woman had been shot.

—In there? Did it frighten you?

I look at him, at his black whiskers, at his patient hands gripping the wheel, at his glances up to the rear-view mirror like a dog diligently aware of a hundred scents at once. I want to hold my camera to his face and say – *Me? Do you think I take pictures of blown-up weddings because I'm easily frightened? Because the body scares me? Do I look like a woman who can't handle blood?* but instead I say – She had her period. I only thought she'd been shot.

Harim and I drive in silence. Outside is a moonscape of desert whizzing past in clouds of tire dust. We overtake mule carts and bands of women on foot carrying firewood.

The truth is that when I saw the blood, deep down I'd wished she'd been shot. The light had angled onto her surfaces in a way that when she lifted her arm to take the piece of cloth, she'd been illuminated like some otherworldly priestess exalting her pagan divinity, her pose a surreal Pieta. Instinctively, I'd reached down for my camera.

Blood must be our scaffolding, not our bones. Without, it we're empty tubes, limp puppets, so I don't believe it's wrong to want to capture that essence on film. So what if I go looking for it, expecting it, craving it? Is it possible to ask if any war photographer is happy in their work? Are we uniquely forbidden from loving what we do? I believe we have the right to inject with aesthetics any cruel reality we want, to frame the truth of human suffering for the distracted world to flip past in magazines on their way to the perfume ads. It's my belief that if you compose a gruesome image with the same intention as a jewelry campaign, people will be more likely to stop and take a long hard look at it.

—Your guy's a riot - a junior cameraman named Remi leans over to me.

—I've got another one - Paul quiets the crowd like a minister - What do lesbians think tampon string is for?

—I don't know, man - Remi is in stitches - What?

—Flossing after eating.

—I don't envy you, Leslie - Greta fails to repress a smirk - Keep your eyes wide open.

You're not married to him yet.

—What? Don't you think that was funny?

—It was a hoot, Paul. You're a douche.

He squints a grin, all teeth and moustache and brown-tinted sunglasses - An anal douche?

Paul's charm has never been his crudity but his ability to get away with it and for people to become more endeared to him because of it. I want to say to Greta, *now he's funny, now's the act that hooks you and makes you want to cling to him forever.* But instead I walk over to the photograph of a Cambodian man being shot point-blank in the side of the head, his eyes grimaced, his black hair blown outward by the blast, and feel worse that it oddly comforts me.

The moon has already descended behind the mountains but its aurora still illuminates the sky behind them, giving the appearance of a cautious, stormy dawn. Distant peaks rise in jagged layers behind the concrete edifices, the streets of the city dark except for the front gate of the mosque where a fluorescent bulb buzzes over the figure of a soldier who has momentarily leaned his head back against the khaki wall. In the distance, a dog barks in sharp falsetto and from the balcony of our room I see the soldier lift his head before resting it back against the wall.

—Do you always smoke? - Harim says from the bed.

—Only after a suicide. I can't think of another occasion it justifies.

—Pleasure?

—Huh... - I inhale - Tell me about what that is. I'm not sure I've ever felt it.

Harim's body is the texture of felt. It is firm and tanned and covered with hair.

—I didn't mean that. I apologize.

—You find death more interesting than happiness?

—As a rule, yes. Death and hatred. I'm attracted to what's consistent in a person.

—Something beautiful has the potential to express more, no? Because it's more rare?

—You're rare – I say – Most men can't express themselves unless they're hating something. Spend an afternoon with my ex-fiancé and you'll know everything he's ever been unhappy about.

—He is a photographer also?

—He's an asshole, but yes, a camera technician. He left me for my best friend. He said he needed someone less grim.

—What is grim?

—Less bothered by the world, more light-hearted. People don't always tell you the truth when they want something. It's amazing what they will say so they can leave something out.

Harim runs his hand up my back onto my neck, palming my skull and gently tugging my hair. His face is an injury of stubble, eyelashes so dark they look dyed – We're not all born to thrive in the same universe – he says – People are like plants that need different recipes of the same nutrients, the same water. You and him sound like separate species.

—We are – I run my fingers through my pubic hair. I should have shaved – Were.

—Is it possible you hate me because I'm also good at something? – Paul lights his cigarette on the bedroom's balcony and blows the smoke out at the galaxy of streetlights tracking Bloor Street into the centre of Toronto.

—Oh, I don't know. Most likely – I unhook my earrings – Most likely, because I'm that bitch that just can't be happy for her partner. Especially when he's crude and inappropriate at absolutely inconceivable times.

Paul sucks at his smoke and exhales through his teeth –
Well, it's funny, Les, because I find it difficult to even look at
you lately. It's horrible to say but I guess it's better now than
later. You're a skeleton, Les. You're addicted to the smell of
blood because you somehow think it's going to one day reveal
to you the meaning of your life. And frankly, I hate having to be
the villain, which is what you always turn me into. Not everyone's your enemy.

—Maybe they are – I say – You are.

As much as *jihad* has been given a bad rap, I admire them
for at least being honest with their hatred. It's always out-
wardly expressed, is what I want to say. Not left to fester in
some stomach vault where it decays into molten clods of resentment that eventually eat through you until they drop out the
bottom. Life is cheap to a terrorist, a more-where-that-comes-
from attitude of wasteful abundance I can't help but envy.

—You're a cunt, Paul.

—And deep down you're demented – he furrows the carpet
with his toes – That's why you try so hard to fix it in me.

—Turn up the sound – Harim instructs – What does this
mean, *tainted love?*

The song buzzes out through dirty speakers on Harim's
shortwave propped in the valley of the bedcovers between us.

—It means something is wrong with your love.

—What could be wrong?

—I don't know – I say – The person who gives it away.
Maybe the one being loved. Maybe their heart is a polluted
river poisoning colonies of goats. Lyrics don't always make

sense. But then again it's difficult to make sense of anything lately.

—Tell me what doesn't make sense – Harim is generously patient and it shows in his over-interest. I churn under his attention.

—I just could never reconcile Paul's façade with who I knew him to be. Like the cake and the icing were incoherent together. I could see through him and he knew this but pretended anyway. And then that bomber pretending she was pregnant. It made me feel sick and I thought I was past that.

—People always pretend – Harim says – We try so hard to be convincing.

—People pretend so they don't feel guilty about failing – I shift onto my side – Paul always said, "*I pretend not to be drunk so I don't feel guilty about not being sober.*" Do you know how infuriating it is for someone to still do that? I mean, to continue to act when they know they're not fooling anyone?

Harim lifts his thick arms, crossing them behind his head – Some people are not comfortable without armour. They're scared of appearing fragile, being taken advantage of.

Furrows of black hair suffocate both armpits. The word *fragile* doesn't seem as though it belongs in his mouth. It assumes an awkward, alien shape and I hope to god he's not going to weep or burst into song. The reason I'm in bed with him now is because he seems so impenetrable, relaxed and secure as a fortress with his face edged in the light from the bedside lamp. Like I could fire a rocket at him and he wouldn't explode. Like it would clang into his chest and drop into the ditch grass, undetonated. I lean over and kiss his mouth and then his neck. I rub my cheek across his chest then bury my nose in his underarm. His coarse hair smells sweet like a field of damp grass; I inhale him as if inhaling earth studded with shrapnel, a roadside crater littered with bush flowers and sun-bleached thighbones, barricades of gnarled sandalwood trees that extend out into the endless scrubland.

The woman must have woken up that morning and tried to eat something. She would have tied the pillow around her stomach and then harnessed herself with the belt of explosives before the sun hit mid-day. She would have felt their calamitous weight hanging from her middle as she walked, peering out from beneath her burka at the grid of the world she would soon splatter herself against. How many hours or days prior had she imagined herself blown to bits, the pieces of her packed against the concrete walls, in the divots where the plastic chair legs met the dusty ground. How often had she thought of the instant she would burst into a constellation like the tails of crimson fire-works igniting outward from one molten core.

—I just need to disappear for several thousand years – I feel him pull me even closer into him – Bury me in sand and forget me, then no one would have to pretend anything.

A camera in lust for images is as dangerous as any bomb. What appeals to me most about photographs is that what gets us closest to the truth is not always so truthful itself. And how it's not always the truth we're even looking for, just something meager and approximate to pacify us in the meantime. Like marriage, martyrdom is a lie: Karbala is hundreds of miles from

Jerusalem, across the most desolate and hostile terrain. Bellies are as likely to be bombs as they are babies, and I've never been much of a deceiver but I've always made my way towards those who are. As much as I believe in the truth of loving, I know I'd become bored with it. That other, more powerful explosions will drift their scalding tentacles across the countryside and intoxicate me beyond reason until I am inspired, revolted and infatuated again.

GLOSSARY

bhajan: Hindu devotional song

dupatta: a long scarf worn by South Asian women

ghat: a series of steps leading down into a body of water

farang: a Thai word that refers to anyone Caucasian

kanji: the adopted logographic Chinese characters used in
modern Japanese writing system.

khao soi: a Thai dish of Burmese descent

longyi: a long piece of cloth used as a skirt or loincloth

mohinga: considered the national dish of Burma

rambutan: a red plum-sized prickly fruit

riel: the currency of Cambodia

Rizla: English brand of cigarette rolling paper

shalwar (or shalwar kameez): loose pajama-liketrousers worn
with a tunic by Pakistani men

sadhu: a Hindu holy man

vairagi: a Hindu renunciate or ascetic

ACKNOWLEDGMENTS

"The Stampede" was published in 2010 in Clark-Nova's anthology *Writing Without Direction: 10½ short stories by Canadian authors under 30*. "That Savage Water" was published in the *Maple Tree Literary Supplement* in 2011. "A Severed Arm" was published in *Lies with Occasional Truth* in 2008. "Les 3 Chevaliers" was published in *Pax Americana* in 2008. "Crawling with Thieves" was published in *The Southernmost Review* in 2009. "The Vagrant Borders of Kashmir" was published in *Nether Magazine* from Mumbai, India, 2012. "Soft Coral, Sinking Pearl" was published in *Cha: An Asian Literary Journal* from Hong Kong in 2012. "A Feast of Bear" was published in *Jonathan* in 2012. "From the Lookout There Are Trees" was published in the anthology *Everything Is So Political* in 2013. "A Fire in the Clearing" and "The Pigeons of Peshawar" appeared, respectively, in the 2013 and 2014 *Carter V. Cooper Short Fiction Anthology–Book 3* and *4*, and in *ELQ/Exile: The Literary Quarterly 37.3 and 39.1*. "Jesus Very Thin and Hungry" appeared in *ELQ/Exile: The Literary Quarterly 38.1*. A hearty thank-you to the editors of these publications.

A special thanks to the Toronto Arts Council and the Ontario Arts Council, without whose support this collection would have taken decades.

For those teachers of risk, craft and imagination: Larry Garber, Rosemary Sullivan, Paul Quarrington, Sarah Kathryn

York, E. Martin Nolan, Graham Arnold, Danielle Van Bakel, Brooke Lockyer, Kate Jenks, Catriona Wright, Jillian Butler, Andrew MacDonald, Michael Collins, Eric Overton, Josip Novakovich, Andrew Battershill, Troy Cunningham, Claire McCague and Jeff Parker. This collection is the brighter because of you.

Effusive thanks to the Exile Editions family whose generosity and enthusiasm are boundless.

Ultimate thanks to my partner, Sergio Beristain, who believed before I did.

Prior to the publication of *That Savage Water*,
Matthew R. Loney was shortlisted twice for

Exile's $15,000 Carter V. Cooper Short Fiction Competition

$10,000 for the Best Story by an Emerging Writer
$5,000 for the Best Story by a Writer at Any Career Point

The 12 shortlisted are published in the annual *CVC Short Fiction
Anthology* series and *ELQ/Exile: The Literary Quarterly*

This annual competition opens in October
details at: www.TheExileWriters.com

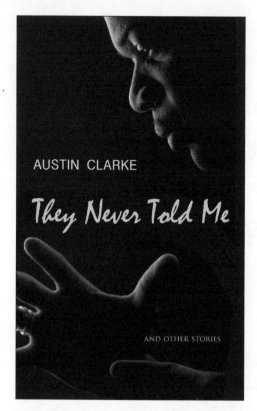

From the winner of the Giller, Commonwealth, Trillium and Writers' Trust prizes, comes an outstanding collection of eight stories.

"[The book has] a fidelity to the kind of sensual language that has always been a hallmark of the author's writing." —*National Post*

"While many of these stories are stationed in memory of the new immigrant experience, the titular story strikes a harmony of hurt as an elderly Barbadian immigrant stumbles around Toronto in black-face, lost in a fog of nostalgia, his struggle with age resurrecting and reciprocating his struggle with racism. The parallel is just the tip of the iceberg of insight Clarke's wisdom offers in these stories."

— *Telegraph Journal*

2013 autumn release   5 × 8   212 pages $19.95

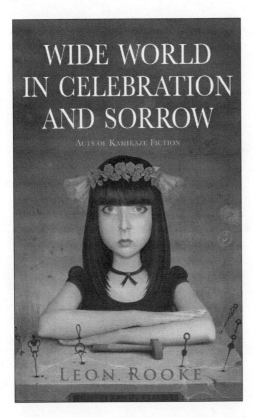

WIDE WORLD
IN CELEBRATION
AND SORROW

ACTS OF KAMIKAZE FICTION

LEON ROOKE

"The 20 pieces that make up *Wide World in Celebration and Sorrow: Acts of Kamikaze Fiction* could be considered a kind of literary tasting menu for those unfamiliar with Rooke's oeuvre... and many of Rooke's signature registers – the absurdist humour, the literary and philosophical allusiveness, the sudden violence – are on display [and...] interact with each other as readily as with a reader."
—*National Post*

2012 autumn release   5.5 × 8.5   272 pages $19.95

"Moreno-Garcia has a spare prose style, but it is one that belies the complexity and depth of her ideas and is well suited to the many common folk who populate her stories. There is a subtlety and seriousness amid the skulls and bones, and beauty among the omens and death." —*The Winnipeg Review*

Spanning a variety of genres — fantasy, science fiction, horror — and time periods, Silvia Moreno-Garcia's exceptional debut collection features short stories infused with Mexican folklore, yet firmly rooted in a reality that transforms as the fantastic erodes the rational.

2012 autumn release   Fiction   5 × 8   224 pages $18.95

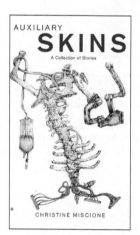

"Miscione excels at writing about horrible things in beautiful ways. Her prose is not only deft and neat, but often wrenchingly lovely, so that much of the text comes across like a suppurating wound wrapped in hand-stitched lace." —*Quill & Quire*

A remarkable first collection. Existing somewhere in that chasm between bodily function and souled-ness, Christine Miscione's debut collection *Auxiliary Skins* illumines all that's perilous, beautiful and raw about being human.

2012 autumn release   Fiction   5 × 8   160 pages $16.95

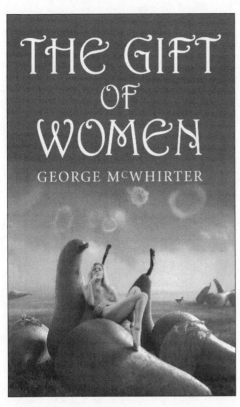

THE GIFT OF WOMEN

OF

WOMEN

GEORGE McWHIRTER

CVC YEARS THREE & FOUR SHORTLISTED

George McWhirter grounds his delightful characters in the real, while his sharp wit and creative scenarios border on the fantastical. A woman adopts a dolphin-man, an Irish madam runs a railroad bordello in the desert, a drought-stricken river joins a jobless man on his way to the pub for a pint of solace, a Catholic woman's seventh child, son of a seventh daughter, is left to the mercy of five convent-schooled sisters. *The Gift of Women* is about sexuality and religion, the surreal and the magical, tales of earthy and incendiary women, capable of setting a man, the Alberni Valley and all of Vancouver Island on fire.

2014 autumn release   5 x 8   256 pages, french flaps $19.95

All books available at www.TheExileWriters.com

Exile's $15,000 Carter V. Cooper Short Fiction Competition

FOR CANADIAN WRITERS ONLY

$10,000 for the Best Story by an Emerging Writer
$5,000 for the Best Story by a Writer at Any Career Point

The 12 shortlisted are published in the annual *CVC Short Fiction Anthology* series and *ELQ/Exile: The Literary Quarterly*

Exile's $2,500 Gwendolyn MacEwen Poetry Competition

FOR CANADIAN & INTERNATIONAL WRITERS

$2,000 for the Best Suite of Poetry
$500 for the Best Poem

Winners are published in *ELQ/Exile: The Literary Quarterly*

These annual competitions open in October
details at: www.TheExileWriters.com